Winter Magic

Winter Magic

A Witch's Yule

SARA HAYDON

Illustrated by Lauren Georgiou

ALLEN&UNWIN

First published in Great Britain in 2024 by Allen & Unwin

Copyright © 2024 by Sara Haydon

Illustrations by Lauren Georgiou

The moral right of Sara Haydon to be identified as the author of this work has been asserted by her in accordance with the Copyright, Designs and Patents Act of 1988.

All rights reserved. No part of this book may be reproduced or transmitted in any form or by any means, electronic or mechanical, including photocopying, recording or by any information storage and retrieval system, without prior permission in writing from the publisher.

No part of this book may be used in any manner in the learning, training or development of generative artificial intelligence technologies (including but not limited to machine learning models and large language models (LLMs)), whether by data scraping, data mining or use in any way to create or form a part of data sets or in any other way.

Neither the publisher nor the author is engaged in rendering professional advice or services to the individual reader. The ideas, procedures and suggestions contained in this book are not intended as a substitute for consulting with your GP. All matters regarding your health require medical supervision. Neither the author nor the publisher shall be liable or responsible for any loss or damage allegedly arising from any information or suggestion in this book.

All names and identifying characteristics have been changed to protect the privacy of the individuals involved.

Allen & Unwin
c/o Atlantic Books
Ormond House
26–27 Boswell Street
London WC1N 3JZ
Phone: 020 7269 1610

www.atlantic-books.co.uk

A CIP catalogue record for this book is available from the British Library.

Designed by Neuwirth & Associates

Hardback ISBN 978 1 80546 282 8
E-book ISBN 978 1 80546 284 2

Printed and bound by CPI (UK) Ltd, Croydon CR0 4YY

10 9 8 7 6 5 4 3 2 1

To my dearest Sylvia, my starlight, may you always believe in the wonders of the world and embrace each moment with boundless love.

Contents

1 Setting the Stage for Yule Magic........ 13
  Exploring Magical Tools............... 14
  Creating Sacred Spaces 34

2 Spirits and Spells of Yule.............. 45
  Dark Tales of Nordic Folklore.......... 46
  Connecting with Deities and Rituals
    for Protection..................... 48
  Spellwork and Book of Shadows 63

3 Feasting and Winter Wishes 75
  Connecting with Community 76
  From Ancient Roots to Modern Tables... 82
  Magic in the Kitchen................. 96

4 Yuletide Divination 105
  Journey with Tarot.................. 106
  Casting Runes 132
  Scrying Mirrors..................... 136

5 A Reflective Journey through Nature ... 147
   The Essence of Elements. 148
   The Guiding Sky. 157
   Light and Lunar Energies 163
   Whispering Woodlands and Their
      Inhabitants. 172

6 Final Thoughts 193

7 Acknowledgements 198

Introduction

I grew up in a household where magic wasn't just a concept, but a part of everyday life. Fairies existed through the sheer power of belief, nightmares were banished with a simple protective kiss on the forehead and, on those weary school journeys, a tight squeeze of the hand was enough to fill your body with sufficient strength to get you home. Now, of course, I recognize all these things as manifestation, protection rituals and energy work... but back then they were simply magic – and that magic exists today, exactly as it did then.

I was brought up in the heart of wintry Finland, where the significance of Christmas transcended mere festivity and is still deeply rooted in folklore and a connection with nature. Nestled in the northern reaches of Europe, Finland experiences long, dark winters, during which communities draw closer, seeking warmth in shared traditions and age-old customs. With the majority of the country being covered by forest and lake, it is a place where nature plays a pivotal role in daily life. Here Christmas time is not simply whimsy, but holds profound significance and is ingrained in our very being. This time of year, ideal for serene contemplation and rest, aligns not only with nature's cycle of rebirth, but also with our own. It presents an opportune moment for awakening curiosity, delving into deeper truths and reflecting on the passage of the year – not to mention uncovering our own unique magic.

In my earlier Christmas memories, my sister and I would warm our hands and feet by the cosy crackling fire as the temperatures in Finland plummeted below freezing. At the heart of the room would stand a tall pine tree that my father had decorated with delicate flickering candles, casting a gentle glow upon the room. Small straw goats, dressed in crimson ribbons, hung alongside handmade ornaments, each whispering tales of ancient lore and casting shadows across the dimly lit room. Our mother, who I always suspected might be a Christmas spirit herself, would

INTRODUCTION

bake in the kitchen, where the air danced with the smell of cinnamon and sugar, making our stomachs flutter with excitement for the feast to come. It was an exciting yet simple celebration, whispering echoes from a bygone era and surreptitiously inspiring one of my greatest passions to come.

This is the story of Yule, the pagan winter festival that will encourage you to connect with your inner nature-witch and craft a magical celebration for yourself and those dearest to you. I wanted to write this book to remind people that you don't have to stop believing in magic just because you grew up. Magic is everywhere you look: it's intertwined in nature, in every river's ripple and in each leaf on a tree, an unseen energy pervading the natural world around us. Magic is what you believe it to be. I know, I know, this sounds far too convenient, but that essence defines its very nature. Sure, the perception of magic varies across cultures, traditions and belief systems, but universally it is about using a deeply personal, intuitive and unique understanding of your experiences to access healing and personal transformation, and to explore the mysteries of existence. Magic is about tapping into different energies and forces to create change, for better or worse.

My own spiritual journey began at eighteen: a seismic shift similar to having a rug pulled from beneath my feet and the veil of reality lifted simultaneously. It challenged everything I knew and sparked an exhilarating curiosity. I delved into the mystical world of tarot, energy work, light work, crystals, shamanism and more, feeling a heightened sense of intuition, a return to primal instincts and a need to align with my soul's path. That, of course, was easier said than done, and, as many of you are probably also all too painfully aware, the layers that had built up over time were strong enough to carry me through another decade of societal conformity. With a master's degree in forensic psychology, I ventured into a career in offender rehabilitation, where I gained true insight into the human psyche and came face-to-face with compelling truths about life and human behaviour. It was the birth of my daughter, however, that sparked the ultimate shift in me – another awakening of sorts. Since then I have collaborated with esteemed psychics and energy healers and have devoted my life to intuitive energy work and transformative tarot, helping thousands of people to gain clarity, guidance and direction on their own personal journeys.

Winter Magic is for anyone seeking to connect with their own magic during the enchanting time of Yule – the pagan festival of the Winter Solstice, which marks the shortest day of the year and is celebrated between 21 and 23 December in the Northern

INTRODUCTION

Hemisphere. It is perfect for those fascinated by history and eager to explore different magical tools and their origins. Whether you are a seasoned practitioner seeking new insights or someone curious to delve into the magical practices associated with this festive season, this book offers a treasury of knowledge and practices to enrich your Winter Solstice celebrations. Come along on the journey through an alternative approach to celebrating the holiday – one that is rooted in Nordic paganism and modern-day witchcraft, where you will be led into a world of mystical practices, rituals, spells, recipes and DIY projects. Discover the art of divination, learn how to perform candle magic, set up your own altar and dive into the captivating world of tarot, crystals, energy healing, moonology, runes and more, while crafting meaningful gifts and goods to enjoy with those nearest and dearest to you.

As winter approaches, many of us prepare to celebrate Christmas, a holiday that is synonymous with joy, present-giving and family gatherings. Yet the origins of this festive season are far older than the Christian holiday and, unknown to many, are rooted in ancient pagan traditions. The celebration that we now know as Christmas was long preceded by Yule – also known as Yuletide or Yulefest and deriving from the Norse word *jól* – a cherished celebration honouring the sun and its increasing light after the Winter Solstice. In many languages, particularly those of the Nordic regions, Christmas is still called by a variation of the word 'Yule': *Jul* in Norwegian, Swedish and Danish; *Joulu* in Finnish; *Joulud* in Estonian; and *Jol* in Icelandic. In Finnish the month itself is called 'Yule month' (*joulukuu*).

Many of the modern-day Christmas traditions, such as decorating a Christmas tree or kissing under the mistletoe, were first performed by the pagans in honour of the Winter Solstice; mistletoe is, in fact, associated with an ancient fertility ritual. In the Northern Hemisphere the sun traces its shortest path across the sky between 20 and 23 December, resulting in the shortest day and the longest night of the year. This astrological occurrence marks the point of the Winter Solstice, signifying the official start to winter and the many rich Yuletide customs. The waning year was, and still is to this day, celebrated by honouring gods, deities and nature itself with festive songs, food, drink, rituals and days of merrymaking.

Many old civilizations celebrated the Winter Solstice. For the Chinese, their annual celebration was called the Dongzhi Festival, meaning 'the arrival of winter', while the Romans had Saturnalia. Cultures around the world had their own ways of honouring the solstice, but Yule was the celebration of the ancient

Scandinavian and Germanic peoples and arguably shaped modern-day Western Christmas traditions the most. Spanning several days, Yuletide was celebrated with colossal bonfires, grand feasts and nights of merry festivities by the fire of the burning Yule log – a carefully selected tree that was burned to ensure warmth throughout the longest night of the year.

Trees were particularly honoured in the north during this time of year, with evergreens being mounted on the corners of homes and a 'Yule tree' either being decorated outside or brought into the house, for protection. The winter months in northern Europe were often a time of food scarcity, and most of the cattle were slaughtered so that the animals would not need to be fed. This temporary abundance of meat meant that it was a good time to feast; and it led to the 'Yule ham' – as much an enticing delicacy as a cherished tradition – whereby a boar was sacrificed to Freyr, goddess of the harvest, who would bless the family with children, love and a bountiful crop in the year ahead. And, as you may have noticed, a ham still adorns many a Christmas table to this day.

*

St Nicholas, a fourth-century AD long-bearded bishop wearing a large cloak, is the figure we now commonly associate with the character of Santa Claus, although the origins of a Santa-like figure are much older. The myth of the sun goddess Beaivi, who was native to the indigenous Sámi people of the northern regions of Norway, Sweden, Finland and Russia, stands out in particular. Beaivi rode a sleigh crafted from reindeer bones, drawn by a white reindeer, and could very well be the original inspiration for Santa Claus and his reindeer. Similarly, the Norse god Odin was described as a bearded old man who rode in the sky with his eight-legged horse Sleipnir. Young children would leave boots filled with carrots and straw outside their doors for Sleipnir to feed on during his 'Wild Hunt' journey through the skies and, in return, would be rewarded with gifts left in their boots… Sound familiar? Legend has it that the god of thunder, Thor, also soared across the skies in his chariot drawn by two flying goats, bestowing gifts upon children. Today, of course, children eagerly anticipate the arrival of Santa Claus, leaving sweet treats for the venerable figure to enjoy during his brief stopover, before waking up to a mound of presents the following morning; or, as occurs in many Nordic countries, on the eve of Christmas, 24 December.

So if evergreens were used in ritualistic practices for health and good fortune, and Odin was in fact the original Santa Claus, how have we become so far removed from the origins of our traditions? The practices and traditions that you'll explore in this book are what would nowadays be referred to as 'pagan', a term initially emerged to describe non-Christian beliefs and cultures. In order to spread Christianity, missionaries journeying across western Europe and beyond sought to abolish many of the 'heathen' pagan practices, rejecting the idea of the people worshipping multiple deities as part of seasonal celebrations. In order to bridge the gap between the different beliefs and cultures, original pagan traditions were incorporated into the new religion. This redirected the purpose of many Yuletide traditions – such as the decoration of a Christmas tree, hanging up a wreath on the door, lighting candles and adorning doorways with mistletoe – away from celebrating the Winter Solstice. Over time, 'Yuletide' became largely synonymous with Christmas, and by the Middle Ages Christianity had almost completely replaced the pagan religions.

With the history of the Vikings gaining in popularity in the twenty-first century, along with a renewed interest in folklore, many people have become more interested in modern paganism, propelling a movement to uncover the roots of our most celebrated traditions. Today growing numbers embark on a profound quest to reclaim the essence of these ancient practices from a more contemporary perspective, breathing life into age-old customs and forging a personal connection with their heritage. While this book serves as a wellspring of inspiration and guidance, its primary purpose is to empower you – the reader – to foster the confidence to embrace and follow your intuition. It is overflowing with occult wisdom, from astrology to alchemy and beyond; and the key to unleashing the full potential of these mystical arts lies not just in reading about them, but in creating a personal relationship with every single practice. So as you delve into these pages, trust your intuition by cultivating a deep awareness of your instincts, and allow yourself the freedom to explore and embrace the transformative journey of your unique path.

Setting the Stage for Yule Magic

Yule magic centres on ancient traditions and sacred tools that illuminate the darkest nights of winter. In this chapter we embark on a journey into the heart of Yule, exploring essential tools and symbols that cleanse, adorn and protect the home during this festive season. From the soft glow of beeswax candles to the fragrant embrace of pine-needle bundles, you'll delve into the art of crafting these magical elements, inviting you to connect with the natural world in a tangible and meaningful way. Discover the significance of candles, evergreens, herbs and more, and learn how to create your own sacred space within the home. From honouring age-old

Yule-tree traditions to performing candle magic with a Yule log, this chapter is a celebration of the transformative power of ritual, whereby through the power of thought, belief and action we align ourselves with the energies of the universe to bring our desires into reality – a practice often referred to as manifestation.

Exploring Magical Tools

Magical tools are objects and instruments used in various spiritual and magical practices to enhance rituals, ceremonies and spellwork. They often hold symbolic significance and are believed to help practitioners focus their intent, connect with spiritual energies and facilitate a deeper connection to the divine or to metaphysical realms. While the specific tools may vary across different magical traditions, some commonly used magical items include athames (ritual knives), wands, chalices, pentacles, candles and crystals. Yule, alongside other pagan holidays, is rich in age-old traditions and tales of magical objects, symbols and tools that enable practitioners to honour this blessed time of rebirth, light and renewal. These elements, which are often closely connected with nature, not only adorn our homes during the darker months, but also serve as conduits of magical energies for protection, rituals and ceremonies during Yuletide.

Below are just a few of the tools and elements that you may wish to bring into your home and incorporate into your rituals. But do remember that starting your own witchy traditions is just as important, so go ahead and incorporate your favourite magical items in order to personalize your pagan celebration.

Candles

Illuminating the path to Yule celebrations, candles symbolize the triumph of light over darkness and have been used symbolically in spiritual rituals across cultures for centuries. They are often thought to represent the eternal flame, a connection to the divine and a beacon of hope in the darkness. In many spiritual traditions, lighting a candle is a symbolic act of seeking enlightenment, and the soft, flickering light mirrors the journey within, enhancing the pathway of self-discovery, clarity and understanding.

Different candle colours hold unique energies, which are chosen based on their correspondence to specific intentions. For example, a white candle symbolizes purity and spiritual enlightenment, while a green candle represents growth and healing. Understanding the significance of colours enhances the spiritual impact of the candles. The act of lighting them during the solstice rituals signifies hope, success and protection, warding off negative energies and inviting in blessings. One of my favourite ways to use a candle during Yuletide is to light a white candle first thing in the morning, to bring calmness and peace into my day. This sets the perfect ambience and lighting for quiet reflection before the hustle and bustle of the day begins.

Here is a table showing the different spiritual meanings associated with various candle colours.

Candle Colour	Representation	Additional Correspondences
White	Purity, spirituality, clarity	Healing, protection, cleansing, peace
Red	Passion, love, courage	Vitality, strength, action
Pink	Romantic love, friendship	Harmony, affection, emotional healing
Orange	Creativity, success, joy	Ambition, optimism, attraction
Yellow	Intellect, communication, confidence	Focus, inspiration, mental clarity

Green	Abundance, growth, healing	Prosperity, fertility, renewal
Blue	Serenity, tranquility, wisdom	Communication, intuition, healing
Purple	Spirituality, psychic abilities, royalty	Ambition, wisdom, divination
Black	Protection, banishing, absorption	Negativity absorption, transition, release
Brown	Grounding, stability, home	Earth-related magic, security, pets
Gold	Wealth, success, achievement	Abundance, luxury, solar energy
Silver	Intuition, reflection, lunar energy	Psychic development, feminine energy, receptivity

Collect the leftover wax from your coloured candles to combine in a candle jar, for a powerful fusion of different intentions, or make your own wax-dipped taper candles from beeswax. Creating hand-dipped candles can be done by repeatedly dipping a wick into melted wax to build up layers to form the candle. The process can be quite time-consuming, although the results are not only beautiful, but also deeply personal and meaningful.

Hand-dipped Beeswax Candles

Materials needed:
1. Wax paper or newspaper
2. Candle wick (cotton braided wick is most common)
3. Scissors
4. Tall container such as a tin can and a saucepan
5. Beeswax
6. Wooden chopsticks (optional)
7. Thermometer
8. Candle dye or colour blocks (optional)
9. Fragrance oil or essential oil (optional)
10. Another tall, narrow container, such as a tin can or a glass
11. Sharp knife (optional)
12. Hairdryer (optional)

Instructions:

Step 1: Prepare Your Workspace

Cover your work area with wax paper or newspaper to protect it from drips and spills. Ensure good ventilation and a stable work surface.

Step 2: Cut Wick to Length

One long wick will be folded and both ends will be dipped in wax to make two candles, so measure and cut your single long wick to be twice the height of your tin can, plus an extra 5 cm. So if your tin can is 10 cm tall, then you would want your wick to be 25 cm long.

Step 3: Melt the Wax

Place your can filled with beeswax into a saucepan of water to create a makeshift double-boiler. The water in the saucepan should come up to about the halfway mark of the can. Melt the beeswax over a low to medium heat. You may find wooden chopsticks useful to mix the wax as it is melting. Use a thermometer to monitor the temperature and aim for the wax to reach 71–77°C, or until it has melted completely.

Step 4: Add Colour and Scent (optional)

If desired, add candle dye or colour blocks to the melted wax to achieve your preferred colour. For fragrance, add fragrance oil or essential oil and mix thoroughly.

Step 5: Dipping the Wick and Shaping

Fill another empty can or a glass with iced water and leave it on the side. Once your wax has melted and reached the desired temperature, start the dipping process. Fold the wick into half, pinching it at the top, and dip both ends of the wick into the wax, allowing it to soak for a few seconds. Lift it out slowly and let any excess wax drip back into the can.

Next, place the dipped wick ends into the iced water. This helps the wax to set quicker. After this, lay your wicks on the counter and gently roll them with your fingers to make them straight and smooth. Skipping this step may result in an uneven and bumpy texture on the finished candle. You don't have to repeat this step after each wax dip – this is simply to ensure that the base layer is smooth.

Step 6: Cooling and Layering

Continue the process of dipping the wicks into wax, and then cold water, until your candles reach the desired thickness. The more dips you do, the thicker the candle will become. If you want a wide candle, this might take numerous dips, so be patient and ensure that each layer hardens before placing the candle back in the wax.

Step 7: Trimming the Candle

Once the candle has reached your desired size and thickness, trim the bottom of the candle with a sharp knife while the wax is still slightly warm. This will ensure a flat end for your candle, but if you wish to keep the candle bottom-end pointy, feel free to skip this step.

Step 8: Final Touches

You may wish to cut the wick and separate the two candles or leave them joined. In addition, you can smooth out any rough spots on the surface of the candle by gently heating the surface with a hairdryer.

Step 9: Curing

Allow the candles to cure and harden completely for at least seventy-two hours before packaging or lighting them.

Evergreens

Working during Yule with verdant foliage and evergreens – such as pine, spruce and holly – is a way to celebrate the enduring life amid the harshness of winter. During the Nordic Yule celebrations, evergreens were often cut and brought indoors to represent the circle of life. They were believed to have power over death because their deep-green colour never faded, and they were used to protect the home and its inhabitants against supernatural forces and death. This practice is still seen today in wreaths.

> *Hang these luxurious branches over your doorways, lay them on the floor of your entranceway or make a wreath to hang on your front door, to repel malevolent energies and invite blessings and prosperity into the home.*

SETTING THE STAGE FOR YULE MAGIC

Below, I've listed some common evergreens with their unique spiritual properties, which you can incorporate into your Yule rituals, decorations and ceremonies.

Pine: Often associated with prosperity, growth and cleansing. Its evergreen nature symbolizes eternal life, while the scent is believed to purify and refresh the spirit.

Spruce: Linked to protection and stability. Its needles are thought to ward off negative energies, making it a symbol of resilience and strength during the Yuletide season.

Fir: Associated with hope, inspiration and transformation. Its branches are used to invoke positive energies and foster a sense of renewal and spiritual growth.

Cedar: Considered a sacred tree in many traditions. It is associated with purification, protection and spiritual strength. Cedar branches or incense are often used for ritual cleansing.

Juniper: Linked to protection and banishing negative energies. It is believed to guard against evil forces and is used in rituals to create a safe and sacred space.

Holly: A symbol of protection and joy. Its vibrant red berries are associated with the life force, and the prickly leaves are thought to repel negativity.

Ivy: Represents endurance, determination and the intertwining of lives. It is often paired with holly to signify the balance between the masculine and feminine energies.

Yew: A tree of transformation and rebirth. It is associated with the cycle of life, death and regeneration. Yew branches may be used to connect with the ancestral spirits during Yule.

Cypress: Linked to purification and transition. It is often used to release and let go of the past, making it a suitable evergreen for Yule rituals focused on renewal.

Common box: Often associated with protection and healing. Its dense evergreen leaves are believed to create a shield against negative energies and promote spiritual well-being.

Herbs and Spices

During Yule, herbs and spices emerge as potent allies in creating powerful rituals and sacred ceremonies. Rosemary, a purifying herb, cleanses, while the warmth and spice of cinnamon and cloves infuse food, drinks and spaces with luck and prosperity. Each herb bears unique properties: juniper is for increasing focus, thyme for courage and bay leaves for powers of divination and wish fulfilment. Whether fresh or dried, these botanicals serve as integral elements in crafting healing stews and invigorating elixirs or as great offerings during rituals.

Among them, frankincense shines brightly during Yule, resonating with the energy of the sun and fire. Honoured across human history, it holds a sacred status, summoning the presence of the divine. Frankincense also holds significance in Christian Christmas traditions, as it was one of the gifts (alongside gold and myrrh) presented by the Magi (the wise men or kings) to the infant Jesus in the story of the Nativity. Many cultures deem frankincense indispensable for elevating spiritual vibrations, and its aroma and smoke are believed to uplift and connect individuals with the higher realms, making it ideal for invoking a sacred atmosphere during Yuletide.

Smudge Sticks and Other Cleansing Tools

Smudging is a ritual used to cleanse places, objects or individuals using the wafting smoke from burning herbs. This ritualistic cleansing removes stagnant energies and prepares the space for sacred work. The smoke acts as a conduit, purifying both the physical and spiritual realms, inviting in positive energies and spiritual clarity.

This winter opt for a different smudging tool – try using a cinnamon stick instead of the traditional white sage or palo santo. Cinnamon, aligned with the planetary energies of Mars and Mercury as well as the element of Fire, offers powerful purification properties. Smudging with a cinnamon stick proves beneficial for manifesting success, enhancing psychic vision and fostering mental clarity.

Here are some of the most commonly used smudging tools for you to try.

White sage: For purification, clearing negative energy and spiritual cleansing.

Palo santo: For purification, attracting positive energy, promoting emotional and physical well-being.

Cedar: For purification, protection, promoting balance and creating a protective energy barrier.

Sweetgrass: For attracting positive energies, blessing a space, promoting harmony and positivity.

If you are looking for smoke-free alternatives to smudging, here are a few options that can offer similar energetic cleansing and purification benefits.

Bells or singing bowls: The resonant tones from bells or singing bowls can help clear stagnant energy and create a harmonious atmosphere.

Crystal cleansing: Selenite is known for its purifying properties. You can use a selenite wand to sweep the energy around a space or over an object.

Salt cleansing: Placing a Himalayan salt lamp in a room is believed to absorb negative energy and create a more positive ambience.

Essential oils: Certain essential oils, such as lavender, sage or cedarwood, can be diffused to purify the air and promote relaxation.

Salt-water cleansing: Mixing sea salt with water and using it as a spray can help cleanse and protect a space without producing smoke.

Moonlight and sunlight: Placing objects or crystals in direct sunlight or moonlight for a few hours can recharge and cleanse their energy. If your altar space doesn't come into direct contact with natural light, you can reflect the sun's or moon's light onto your altar space using a mirror.

Bells

Ever wondered where the saying 'saved by the bell' comes from? Bells, with their harmonious tones, would traditionally be rung in the mornings during Yule to chase away the demons and other dark entities that arise during the darkest night of the year. They are still a recognizable Christmas decoration, and the familiar red-and-white Christmas hats, particularly those worn in Nordic countries, are often adorned with bells. They serve to protect the threshold between the earthly and spiritual realms, so why not hang some bells on your door this year to signal the entrance to a sacred space?

> *Hang a bell or two in your bedroom window to help ward off nightmares and invite in benevolent spirits for protection.*

Nature's Treasures

During the Winter Solstice tokens of abundance, such as nuts, seeds, berries, fruit and evergreen plants, embody the promise of renewal. Adorn altars and wreaths with pine cones, symbolizing growth and enlightenment. Use vibrant berries such as holly and mistletoe, hanging them from door frames and incorporating them into the bedroom décor, for fertility and a deeper connection with your partner.

> *Collect some fallen pine cones to sit on your nightstand, or pop an acorn in your pocket as a talisman for the day.*

Pine-Needle Bundles

Pine needles, which are plentiful in Nordic countries, signify resilience, renewal, purification, connection to nature, protection and healing. They are often incorporated into rituals, ceremonies and decorations to harness these symbolic energies. Craft a small pine-needle bundle to sit on your altar and remind you that, even during the dark days of winter, life persists in the face of adversity, heralding the return of light. It is not recommended to use them as smudging sticks, but if you wish to work with pine's ritualistic smoke you can burn them in a fireplace or a campfire, as you would firewood.

Materials needed:

1. **Pine needles** (gather fresh, fragrant pine needles, preferably from pine trees known for their resilience and therapeutic properties, such as the Scots pine.)

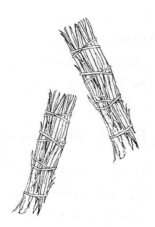

2. **Twine or cotton thread** (natural fibres work best to bind the bundles)

3. **Scissors** (to trim and shape the bundles)

Instructions:

Step 1: Preparation

Select fresh pine needles, ensuring they are free from damage or discoloration. Aromatic varieties, such as Weymouth pine or Scots pine, work well. Gather a generous handful of needles, as you'll need enough to form a compact bundle.

Step 2: Align the Needles

Lay the pine needles on a clean surface, arranging them in a uniform direction. This helps to create a tidy and cohesive bundle. Remove any stray needles or debris to ensure a neat appearance.

Step 3: Bind the Bundle

Gently gather the pine needles, ensuring they are aligned, and hold them firmly together at one end. Take your twine or cotton thread and start binding the bundle tightly, wrapping it around the gathered end in a criss-cross pattern. Secure the thread with a knot.

Step 4: Shape the Bundle

Trim any excess length from the bound end to create a tidy and even appearance. Use scissors to shape the bundle into a compact and visually appealing form. Ensure the needles are held firmly together without any loose ends.

Step 5: Dry and Infuse Your Intentions

Hang the newly crafted pine-needle bundles in a well-ventilated area, away from direct sunlight, to dry. As they do so, they will emit their invigorating aroma, infusing your space with the scent of the forest. While they dry, imbue them with your intentions – protection, renewal or purification – by holding them and focusing on your desired energy. Once you have done this, they are ready to be placed on your altar.

Straw Goats

Straw goats traditionally hold deep significance during Yule in Nordic and Northern European countries, and still do in modern-day celebrations. In the Swedish town of Gävle a giant straw goat has been built every year since 1966 and is still frequently burned down by the townspeople (it now has a twenty-four-hour guard to prevent would-be arsonists). The Finnish word for Father Christmas, *Joulupukki*, literally translates as 'Christmas goat', because gifts were traditionally brought by the Yule goat, rather than by the Santa Claus we all recognize today.

The goat is believed to originate from the tale of Thor's chariot goats, symbolizing resilience, strength and protection. The goat can also be seen as significant during Yule as the sun enters the astrological sign of Capricorn (depicted as a goat) during the celestial event of the Winter Solstice in the Northern Hemisphere. Ruled by Saturn, the earth element of Capricorn marks a period of reflection, preparation and renewal, encouraging us to harness the strength and determination of the goat as we transition into a new season. The Yule goat, adorned with ribbons and bells and hung in homes, ensures prosperity and guards against misfortune, while also promoting a good harvest in the upcoming year.

> *A popular Christmas prank in old Scandinavian society was to hide a goat ornament, or another object made of straw, in a neighbour's home. After finding the object, the neighbour would then go on to do the same in the next house along. Why not try this playful tradition and see whose goat ornament can stay hidden the longest?*

Creating Sacred Spaces

Yule Tree

While it was a common pagan tradition to bring a Yule tree inside the home, people in Nordic countries originally decorated a tree outside, due to an abundance of forested areas. These trees were embellished with foraged ornaments such as pine cones, nuts, berries, fruits, and even coins, symbolizing abundance and prosperity. Doing this was considered an offering to the creatures of the land, providing sustenance to birds, squirrels and other wildlife, while also manifesting abundance for the year to come. The branches of pine, fir, cedar, juniper or spruce were also adorned with hanging candles and various ornaments, representing the radiant light of the sun, moon and stars.

If you don't have a tree to decorate outside, consider skipping the commercial decorations this year and instead venture outdoors to forage for natural elements to bring into your home.

Arranging Your Altar

Crafting a sacred Yule altar serves as a powerful way to honour the season's significance, embrace the symbolism of light and nature and foster a deeper spiritual connection with the time of year. As you create your altar, infuse it with your intentions, gratitude for the returning light and reverence for the enduring spirit of nature. A personalized altar is a meaningful space for you to conduct any rituals and practices that you wish to carry out this Yuletide, so use this space to lay out your favourite spiritual tools, such as tarot cards, singing bowls and crystals.

Prior to building your altar, orient it to face northwards using a compass, to align with the Yule energies. Earth is the north's corresponding element, and here it signifies stability and grounding, as well as connection to our physical selves and the world around us. Aligning your altar in this direction also honours the geographical north and its spirits. In contrast, you may wish to turn your altar to face east if you want to honour the rising sun and the increasing light during Yule.

I always recommend smudging your space before starting to build your altar. Negative energy can often accumulate over time, leading to potential harm. The persistent presence of negative energy can create an environment where negative thought patterns or behaviours start to become more noticeable. Over time, this accumulation can contribute to chronic stress, irritability, headaches and other manifestations of an imbalance within your environment and, subsequently, within you as well. Importantly, failing to cleanse your altar space before building on it might disrupt or hinder the flow of positive energy, potentially diminishing the effectiveness of your rituals and intentions.

When selecting which items you want to place on your altar, be conscious of your colour choices and consider ones that embody the essence of Yule. Gold represents the return of the sun, symbolizing vitality, warmth and prosperity. Green signifies nature's enduring spirit and health, while white represents purity, symbolic of the snowy landscape often observed in the

Northern Hemisphere. Choose appropriate colours for your altar cloth, candles and any other objects that you wish to place on your altar, keeping in mind the spiritual properties of each colour (see page 16).

Consider incorporating solar symbols, such as anything circle-, cross- or spiral-shaped, in copper or gold. These shapes represent the sun deities such as Ra (Egyptian mythology) and Surya (Hindu mythology), who are both often depicted with a sun disc and celebrate the rebirth of light and life, inviting vitality into the space. Arrange these symbols on or around the altar centre, which commonly holds a source of light, either a Yule log with candles or a lantern.

Don't forget to adorn your altar with your favourite nature elements, such as moss, evergreen branches, pine cones, holly berries, mistletoe, acorns or the charming pine-needle bundles that you created earlier. Finally, incorporate a bowl of water to represent nature's life-giving force and to balance the energies of Fire on your altar.

Tips for Altar Arrangement

- ✦ **Position items with intention** by bringing mindful awareness, purpose and focus to your actions. When trying to be more intentional, aim to clarify your purpose, stay present in the moment, visualize your success in whatever you are doing and emotionally connect to your goal. Aim to create a harmonious and balanced layout for your altar.

- **Arrange candles and symbols** to radiate outwards from the central light source, signifying the spreading of light and blessings.

- **Consider adding crystals** like citrine or clear quartz for amplified energy and clarity.

- **Utilize sacred geometry** or symbols that are meaningful to your spiritual practice to enhance the altar's energy.

Yule Log

The Yule log traces its roots to ancient pagan customs across Europe, symbolizing the celebration of the Winter Solstice and the return of light. This belief holds rich symbolism, embodying the warmth of community and family-oriented Yuletide activities.

Harvesting a Yule log traditionally required obtaining a tree as a gift or cutting one from your own property, as it was considered unlucky to purchase it. On the eve of the Winter Solstice the log was placed (larger end first) into the hearth of your home, where it would then gradually be fed into the fire throughout Yuletide until the whole of it had burned, which could take up to twelve days. Families would decorate the tree with pine cones, ivy, holly and evergreens, and a fragment of the log was preserved and placed beneath a bed as protection against misfortune, fires or lightning. The next year, this remaining piece kindled the fire for the new Yule log. Failing to light the new log on the first attempt was considered an ill omen, suggesting potential misfortune for the household.

While a burning log in the middle of the living room might be considered a bit of a fire hazard, many people choose to honour this old tradition by bringing in a much smaller log and decorating this instead. Due to their properties of strength, protection and new beginnings, common choices for the Yule log wood are oak, ash or birch. Decorate your Yule log with cinnamon sticks, evergreen branches, holly, mistletoe or dried fruits such as oranges and apples, but don't be limited to the traditional ornaments; and incorporate your own practices into welcoming home your Yule log, such as carving or painting protective sigils onto the bark. If possible, drill or carefully carve out holes in the log for tea lights or candle sticks, to represent light and bring warmth to your home. Consider placing the log on your dining-room table, as feasting would traditionally be in full swing while the traditional Yule log burned. Alternatively, position it at the centre of your altar and surround it with more candles, crystals or other items that align with your Yule intentions, creating a harmonious space for other rituals to be carried out.

CANDLE MAGIC RITUAL FOR YOUR YULE LOG

The ancient practice of candle magic has been used to capture the essence of intention-setting and manifestation across cultures and traditions for thousands of years. Candles are believed to serve as conduits for focused energy and, at its core, candle

magic revolves around the principle that energy follows intention. The process involves focusing on a specific goal or desire while lighting the candle. The flame then becomes a visual representation of your aspirations, creating a sacred space to manifest intentions and send them out into the universe. The candle itself represents the element of Fire, symbolizing transformation and change. In spiritual alchemy, fire is the catalyst for turning base materials into gold, representing the process of spiritual evolution and enlightenment. It signifies the inner alchemical journey towards higher states of consciousness.

Some Applications of Candle Magic

- **Manifestation rituals:** Use candle magic for manifesting desires or goals, visualizing the desired outcome as the candle burns.

- **Healing practices:** Channel energy for healing by directing your intentions towards the candle flame, visualizing wellness and vitality.

- **Protection and cleansing:** Cleanse spaces or invoke protective energies by burning candles with corresponding intentions.

Materials needed:

1. Candle (choose a candle that is safe to hold and doesn't get too hot)
2. Matches or a lighter

3. A Yule log (you can chop your own log from a tree, ask for one as a gift or, these days, purchase one)

4. A pen and paper

Instructions:

Step 1: Colour Symbolism

Begin by choosing the candle for your Yule log. Each candle colour carries unique vibrations. Red signifies passion and vitality, while green embodies growth and abundance. Using the chart on page 16, choose the colours that resonate with your intention for the ritual.

Step 2: Cleanse the Candle

Pass the candle through incense smoke or consecrate it with prayers or affirmations, asking any attached energy to remove itself and visualizing pure cleansing energy entering the candle's core.

Step 3: Charge the Candle

Hold the candle, meditate and focus your thoughts, infusing the candle with your intentions and desires (such as healing, abundance, love, money, protection or strength). Carve or write symbols, words, runes or sigils (see page 51) into the wax to enhance the candle's energy and connection to your intention, or simply write your intentions on a piece of paper and place it underneath your Yule log.

Step 4: Ignite the Flame

Light the candle, acknowledging the spark of energy and the connection between the physical and spiritual realms. Focus on your intention manifesting as the flame grows stronger and starts to flicker.

Step 5: Power of Closure

Conclude your candle magic ritual by letting the candle burn out completely or snuffing it out, with the intention that the spell or ritual has been sealed. Dispose of the remaining wax or remnants appropriately, honouring the energy and intention that you have channelled.

Spirits and Spells of Yule

The Winter Solstice is a time when the veil between the worlds grows thin, revealing the dance between darkness and light. From the chilling whispers of Yule monsters to the comforting embrace of protective deities, in this chapter we will explore runes, unlock the power of personalized sigils, delve into the transformative realm of energy work and craft your own Nordic decorations for protection. You'll also learn the basics of spellwork and embark on a journey of empowerment as you start your very own 'Book of Shadows'.

Dark Tales of Nordic Folklore

Different cultures across the world have their own ways of marking the Winter Solstice. Due to the recurring themes of life, death and rebirth associated with the celebration, Yule is rich in legendary tales of both light and dark entities and spirits. The Vikings considered the solstice a time when the veil between the dead and the living was at its thinnest. They would offer food and drink to their ancestors, believing that the spirits of the departed would return home to celebrate with them. In what is now Scandinavia, Odin – revered as the all-father in Norse mythology – held immense importance in Yule celebrations, leading a ghostly procession through the skies on Yule night, looking to gather souls of the recently deceased to add to his ranks. Witnessing or hearing Odin's 'Wild Hunt', however, was considered a bad omen and a foretelling of disasters to come.

One of the ways in which the Wild Hunt is celebrated today is by taking a walk through the forest during the day and then running the same path come nightfall. If you can navigate the route swiftly in the dark you will have gained the trust of the woodland spirits and may be permitted to cut down trees for your personal use.

> *Take a stroll in the forest as the sun starts to wane on the day of the Winter Solstice and pay close attention to the sounds in the skies. While you may not hear Odin's procession, focus your attention on what you can hear. Take a moment to be mindful of nature's sounds and hear what the wind has to whisper.*

There are many variations of the Wild Hunt, and many other entities and gods were said to lead it, including Lussi, a female demon or witch, marking Lussi Night on 13 December in Norway and Sweden. Between Lussi Night and Yule it was believed that trolls, malevolent spirits and departed souls roamed the lands. Lussi Night was seen as perilous, especially for mischievous children, as the legend had it that Lussi would descend down the chimney to claim those who had misbehaved. *Lussevaka* was the custom of staying awake throughout Lussi Night to guard the household and the family – and modern-day festivities now involve parties celebrating until dawn.

Connecting with Deities and Rituals for Protection

Beyond the Northern Hemisphere, various cultures and traditions harbour their own tales of dark entities during Yule. From ghostly apparitions to giant monsters, these stories speak of a time when the natural and the supernatural merge together. Possibly one of the most well-known Yuletide monsters is the Krampus, a horned demonic figure from Central European folklore, who would punish misbehaving children during the Yule season. Amid these ominous stories, it is important to remember that Yule is not solely a tale of darkness. It embodies a harmony of light and shadow, where the comfort and closeness of community shield against the darker forces and negative energies. Delve into these shielding practices to ensure that you are up to date with your magical self-defence and to harmonize yourself with positive and protective energies.

Harnessing Protective Runes

Nordic runes (also known as Viking runes or Norse runes) are part of the runic alphabet systems used by early Germanic tribes, particularly the Norse people. Runic alphabets evolved over time and have had a variety of uses throughout history, from writing to divination. The most well-known runic alphabet is the Elder Futhark, which consists of twenty-four characters. These runes have symbolic meanings and are considered sacred and powerful in ancient Norse culture, being associated with, for example, protection, guidance, communication and wisdom.

In more modern times each rune holds a unique significance and is used for various spiritual or magical practices, including spellwork and meditation. Algiz (which represents protection against malevolence) and Thurisaz (defence) are great runes to consider using during this time of year. Algiz, resembling the antlers of an elk, signifies a protective divine connection, while Thurisaz, which resembles a thorn, wards off unwanted energies. They are both commonly hung on doors and windows to fortify the energetic boundaries of the home.

Bindrunes combine multiple runes, synergizing their powers into a single symbol. For instance, a bindrune merging Algiz and Thurisaz offers a

fortified shield against negativity. There are many different ways in which you may want to use bindrunes for personal protection. The most common ways to lay out your bindrunes are:

- **Stacked bindrunes:** Two or three runes laid one on top of the other along a shared axis.

- **Same-stave bindrunes:** A series of runes connected along a common line placed either horizontally or vertically.

- **Radial bindrunes:** Each rune is placed on the end of a rod, radiating outwards from a common centre point.

To create a bindrune, select runes corresponding to your protective intent and blend them together, channelling their combined energies.

Unlocking Your Own Sigils

Sigils are more than just symbols; they are conduits of intention, personalized emblems representing a specific purpose or desire. When it comes to protection, they become powerful talismans, embodying a shield against negative energies. Crafting a protective sigil begins with a clear and precise intention for the safeguarding that you seek. It might involve safeguarding your home, shielding against negative influences or promoting a sense of personal safety. Whatever your intention may be, condense it into a concise statement or phrase.

Next, pick out the key words from this phrase that encapsulate the main elements of your intention: for instance, your key words might be 'home,' 'safety' and 'security'. From the key words, extract the most critical letters. This could be the initial letters of each key word or a combination of letters that resonate with you. Using the example above, you might extract H, S and S. These are the building blocks of your sigil, which you then merge to create a unique new symbol. The design can include lines, curves or shapes, but the key is to craft it in a way that deeply aligns with your protective intent.

Once you've finalized your sigil design, it's time for activation. Find a serene space where you can focus without distractions. Centre yourself, concentrate on your protective intention and hold the sigil in your mind's eye. Trace or draw it on a piece of paper or on any medium that feels right to you, all the while infusing it with your energy and your intent. Envision the sigil radiating with protective energy, forming a shield around you or your space. This act charges the sigil with your focused intent, making it a potent talisman for protection.

Whether you choose to draw it on a protective amulet and wear it, or on a piece of paper and keep it hidden, the charged sigil serves as a constant reminder of your intention and the protective energy you have invested in it. Regularly reconnect with your sigil to reinforce its power and remind yourself of the protection it offers.

Easing into Energy Work

Energy work refers to various practices that involve manipulating or channelling the body's energy to promote physical, emotional or spiritual well-being.

It is based on the concept that all living beings possess an energy field or life force, which is often referred to as chi, prana or life energy. Some of the most well-known modalities of energy work include:

- **Reiki:** A Japanese technique that involves the laying-on of hands to promote healing and relaxation by channelling energy.

- **Qigong:** An ancient Chinese practice that combines movement, breath and meditation to cultivate and balance the body's energy.

- **Acupuncture/acupressure:** Methods from Traditional Chinese Medicine (TCM) that involve stimulating specific points on the body to balance the flow of energy.

- **Crystal healing:** Using crystals to absorb, amplify and direct energy in the body for healing and balance.

- **Chakra balancing:** Focusing on the body's seven energy centres (chakras) to promote balance and healing by removing blockages.

- **Aura cleansing:** Clearing and balancing the aura – the energy field that surrounds the body – to maintain overall well-being.

All of these modalities can be useful in protecting yourself against negative energies or replenishing your energy storage during Yule. However, many of them take years of practice to master. A very quick and easy way to protect your energy is through what I like to call 'energy bathing'. Start off by gently rubbing the palms of your hands together for about a minute, as though you are trying to warm them. Once you feel a sufficient amount of heat between your palms, move your hands a few centimetres apart. Next, bring your palms closer together again, but do not let them touch, before pulling them further apart once more. Repeat this until it feels as if, when you are bringing your palms together, a concrete mass starts to gather between them. It might feel like pressure or resistance, but, once you notice it, focus on the sensation and the form it takes. If you are very good at visualizing, you may even want to try to fling this energy mass from one hand to another, like a ball.

When you are confidently holding energy in the palms of your hands, visualize the surface of the energy becoming reflective, like a tinted window – just reflective enough to let the positive intentions in, but keep the negative ones out. Now charge the energy with any thought you choose (perhaps an intention of protection or positivity), before raising your hands and splashing it on your face, as you would do with water. Draw your hands above and over your head, covering as much surface area as you can. Remember that the most effective protection comes from rituals performed with focused intention and belief in their power to shield against darkness. Adjust and adapt this practice to resonate with your own personal beliefs.

Guardian Spirits and Enchanted Beings

Amid the haunting stories of Yule monsters, there are protective guardian spirits and enchanted beings that come alive, offering balance to some of the darker tales of Yule. Among these intriguing stories, creatures such as the *tonttu* (Finnish gnome-like Yule creatures), the *haltija* (Finnish elven-like spirits) and gods and goddesses emerge as guardians and protectors during this magical time. During Yule, it is customary to acknowledge and respect these guardian spirits through rituals, offerings and acts of gratitude. By fostering these ethereal bonds, communities honour the protective presence of various folklore figures, embracing their wisdom and guidance into the New Year.

Hailing from Nordic folklore, the *tonttu* stands as a cherished household spirit, especially during

Yule. Often depicted as small, gnome-like creatures sporting a white beard and a red knitted cap, these beings are believed to reside in nooks and crannies within homes, barns and forests. Known for their benevolence, *tonttus* take on the role of caretakers, safeguarding the household, animals and even the land itself. At Yuletide families leave out offerings of food or drink, such as porridge or a bowl of grains, to honour these creatures. It is believed that nurturing a harmonious relationship with the *tonttus* brings good fortune, protection and prosperity to the household throughout the festive season.

Alongside the mystical gnomes of the North, the Norse mythological pantheon features most prominently during Yuletide. Freyja, the radiant goddess of love and fertility, graces Yule with her hope and rejuvenation, marking the promise of new beginnings and fertility. Freyja also possesses magical abilities, specifically the gift of *seiðr*, a form of Norse magic associated with prophecy and the manipulation of fate. Odin rides across the skies on Sleipnir, bestowing blessings and joy upon the season, while Frigga, the queen of the gods and Odin's wife, who declared mistletoe a plant of love (despite it killing her son), embodies love, sacrifice and the cycle of rebirth. As the protector of both gods and mortals, Thor had a boisterous spirit that signifies resilience against the harsh winter elements, ensuring safety and security during the festivities.

> *Did you know that Thursday is named after Thor, the hammer-wielding Norse god of thunder? In Old English, Thursday is called Thunresdæg, which means 'Thor's day', and you may wish to leave out mead, ale or bread as an offering to him on this weekday – even better if this occurs during a thunderstorm.*

Guardians of Nature

Embedded in Finnish folklore, *haltija* are supernatural beings akin to sprites or fairies, each of which is aligned with the protection and well-being of nature and its inhabitants. These spirits are believed to inhabit forests, streams and natural landmarks, much like nymphs, offering guardianship over their respective domains. *Haltijas* safeguard travellers, guide lost souls and protect the natural world, and their presence is celebrated through offerings and rituals in exchange for their protective blessings.

Types of *Haltijas* Associated with Yule

- *Metsänhaltija* **(forest spirits):** Guardians of the forest, these spirits are linked to trees, plants and wildlife. During Yule, offerings of nuts, berries and seeds honour them.

- *Vedenhaltija* **(water spirits):** Dwelling in lakes, rivers and streams, these spirits are honoured during Yule with offerings of water, fish and grains.

- *Talonhaltija* **(house spirits):** Protecting homes and hearths, these beings are revered with offerings such as bread, salt or grains placed in the home during Yule.

- *Saunahaltija* **(sauna spirits):** Linked to the sauna, these spirits are honoured with birch branches and sap, salt, aromatic herbs and even beer.

- *Pellonhaltija* **(field spirits):** Connected to cultivated lands, crops, and harvest, these beings are revered with offerings of grains such as barley, as well as fruits and vegetables.

- *Ilmanhaltija* **(air spirits):** Associated with the wind and air, these spirits are honoured with feathers, incense and wind chimes.

> *Did you know that J. R. R. Tolkien drew upon Finnish mythology and language for inspiration in creating the elvish language Quenya, which is spoken by the elves in his famous epic fantasy series* Lord of the Rings? *He also used the epic* Kalevala, *a nineteenth-century compilation of Finnish mythology that is abundant with* haltijas, *to shape the world of Middle Earth.*

A *Traditional* Himmeli

Another way to connect with the Nordic spirits and traditions is to craft a handmade *himmeli*: a traditional mobile made from reeds or straw, bound together with string, often forming geometric shapes and sometimes further decorated with items such as wood, yarn or feathers. Deriving from the German and Swedish words *himmel*, meaning 'sky' or 'heaven', the *himmeli* ornament is known by many names, such as the Estonian *jõulukroon*, which translates as 'Yule crown'. The base of a traditional *himmeli* consists of twelve fragments symbolizing the twelve months of the year, and it is customarily hung up at Yule and kept until the sun starts to wane again at the Summer Solstice in June – which is also celebrated across the Nordic countries.

Himmelis are hung up as an offering to the crop and field spirits to ensure a good harvest the following year, and it is thought that the larger the *himmeli*, the better the next year's rye crop will be. Beyond ensuring a bountiful harvest, *himmelis* are hung above the main dining area of the house to trap negative energies and evil spirits and to safeguard homes, manifesting luck and blessings to its residents.

A Protective *Himmeli*

Materials needed:

1. Four paper straws (of average length of about 20 cm)

2. Scissors

3. Needle/string and thread, cut into a 160 cm length (or longer if you plan on adding in more layers to the *himmeli*)

4. Measuring tape (optional)

SPIRITS AND SPELLS OF YULE

Instructions:

Step 1: Cut the Straws

Measure and cut the four paper straws into three pieces of equal length.

Step 2: Thread the Straw

Take a piece of thread or string and pass it through the first straw piece, then thread the other two straw pieces onto the string, ensuring that they are side by side and snug against each other.

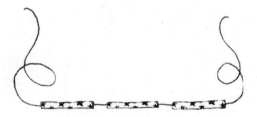

Step 3: Form the First Triangle

Once all three straw pieces are on the string, bring both strings together, forming a triangle, and tie a knot using both strings. Leave one of the string ends long, because this is where the other straws will be threaded through.

Step 4: Form the Second Triangle

Add two more pieces of straw to create a second triangle and tie.

Step 5: Form Triangles Three, Four and Five

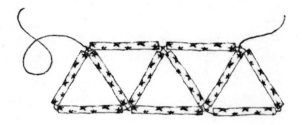

Repeat Step 4 until you have just one piece of straw left.

Step 6: Secure and Shape

Add on the final piece of straw and tie the string coming through it to the short string left loose on the first triangle.

Step 7: Finish

Finish off your *himmeli* by cutting an extra piece of string and threading it through the corners of your two loose triangles, so that you bring their corners together to make a diamond shape.

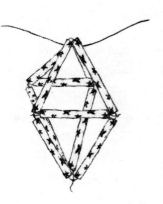

Step 8: Thread and Decorate

Get creative! You can incorporate more shapes, add beads or even paint your *himmeli* to suit your taste.

Spellwork and Book of Shadows

The Winter Solstice is a particularly potent time to practise spellwork, because many practitioners believe that the alignment of celestial energies during this time of year can enhance the effectiveness of spells. On the one hand, the solstice marks the beginning of winter and the period of rest, creating the opportune time for spellwork focused on personal reflection; and on the other, it represents the birth of the sun, making spells crafted around personal growth, transformation and new beginnings especially powerful.

When we think of spellwork, often the first thing that comes to mind is people dramatically waving wands, muttering incantations and making objects levitate. In reality, spell-casting is a far more personal and subtle process. At its core, spellwork is the art of utilizing focused intention, energy and rituals to bring about change in the physical or spiritual realm. Spells can be as simple as whispered affirmations or as elaborate as carefully crafted ceremonies, but their beauty lies in their versatility, offering practitioners a diverse toolkit with which to address different aspects of their lives.

Before we delve into what spellwork really is, we should first have a look at what it is not. It is important to understand the different uses of spellwork and to break free of any stereotypes that might be tied to the practice, before embarking on your own journey with the craft. Witchcraft does not equal spell-casting. While spellwork is a component of some magical practices, it does not define the entirety of witchcraft. Witchcraft encompasses a diverse range of spiritual and magical traditions, and not all practitioners engage in spellwork. Likewise, not all people who engage in spellwork identify as practising witchcraft.

Another big misconception associated with spellwork is that it is exclusively used for dark magic with malevolent intentions and is automatically linked to evil and demonic spirits. In truth, spellwork covers a wide range of practices that focus on positive goals such as healing, self-improvement and personal empowerment, with practitioners frequently concentrating on promoting positive energy, balance and harmony. Lastly, if you are expecting instantaneous tangible results, you may wish to reconsider your idea of the concept. In reality, spells often take time to manifest, and the outcomes may be subtle. It's crucial to approach spellwork with an open mind and to understand that patience and the power of belief play significant roles in the practice.

Let's take a look at some essential elements of spellwork and how you can start to practise and personalize your craft. Spellwork often involves the use of tools such as candles, crystals, herbs and incense, so consider which tools you have available. While it's beneficial to assess the tools you have to hand, remember that you don't need to make new purchases to engage in spellwork. Working with natural elements, household and garden items, pantry ingredients and home-made creations can be just as powerful as traditionally recognized tools such as crystals and incense.

Always begin by clarifying your intentions. What do you seek to manifest or transform? Whether it's love, abundance, protection or healing, a clear and specific intention forms the foundation of effective spellwork. Many practitioners use correspondences – associations between colours, herbs, crystals and celestial events – to enhance the potency of their spells. For example, to cultivate courage and strength, a practitioner might use red candles (symbolizing bravery), ginger (associated with strength) and tiger's-eye crystals (known for fostering confidence) and work with them during the Full Moon, when the heightened energy is thought to intensify the effects of the spell and contribute to its success. Research the correspondences that align with your intention and incorporate them accordingly to make your spells work better.

Lastly, consider the timing of your spells. Lunar phases, days of the week, astrological events and even the time of day can influence the energy available for your work. Consider the specifics of the spells that you intend to perform and align them with favourable times.

Tips for Effective Spellwork

Clarity and focus: Before casting a spell, cultivate a clear and focused mind. Meditate on your intention and visualize your desired outcome. Ensure that your thoughts and emotions are aligned with your purpose.

Respect for free will: When crafting spells that involve others, respect their free will. Focus on influencing situations rather than individuals, allowing space for ethical considerations.

Gratitude and release: Express gratitude after casting a spell, acknowledging the energy and forces at play. Release the attachment to the outcome, trusting that the universe will manifest your intentions in the way that things are meant to unfold.

Record your journey: Keep a magical journal to document your spells, their outcomes and your personal reflections. This practice not only enhances your connection with the craft, but also serves as a valuable resource for future spellwork.

Starting Your Own Book of Shadows

You may have heard the word 'grimoire', originating from the French *grammaire*, meaning 'a work written in Latin'. A grimoire is a book, often with magical or occult content, that contains instructions for rituals, spells and other esoteric knowledge. Grimoires used to be, and still are, a way to share magical knowledge and pass it down the generations, and archaeologists have discovered magical incantation engravings dating back as far as the fourth or fifth century AD. The terms 'Book of Shadows' and 'grimoire' are often used interchangeably, but historically they have different connotations and uses. The 'Book of Shadows' is often associated with modern neo-pagan nature-based religions such as Wicca; it was popularized by Gerald Gardner, one of the founders of Wicca in the mid-twentieth century, and is typically a personal and reflective journal documenting the practitioner's personal experiences, thoughts, spells, rituals and magical experiments. The Book of Shadows is considered to be an evolving record of your spiritual journey, whereas a grimoire is traditionally more of an instruction manual containing specific instructions for performing rituals, casting spells and invoking magical entities.

Creating a Book of Shadows is a deeply personal and intuitive process, and the Winter Solstice – symbolizing introspection and reflection – is the perfect time to start your own. There is no right or wrong way to document your journey, as long as it feels right to you. Saying that, here are some tips that might make it easier for you to begin it.

Select your book: Choose a special notebook or journal for your Book of Shadows. It can be leather-bound, handmade or any book that resonates with you.

Set your intentions: Before you start, set intentions for your Book of Shadows. Clarify its purpose – whether it's for spells, rituals, reflections or a combination.

Create sections: Organize your Book of Shadows into sections. Common sections include spells, rituals, correspondences, divination and personal reflections.

Gather information: Collect information that aligns with your magical practice. Include correspondences, symbols, moon phases, herbs, crystals and any other relevant details.

Write clearly: Write in a clear and understandable manner. Use your own words, and be specific in detailing each spell or ritual. Include instructions, steps and intentions.

Incorporate your experiences: Share personal experiences, both successes and failures. This adds authenticity to your Book of Shadows and serves as a reference for future work.

Include artwork: Enhance your Book of Shadows with illustrations, symbols or drawings. This adds a visual and creative element to your magical record.

Regular updates: Treat your Book of Shadows as a living document. Regularly update it with new insights, spells or experiences. This ensures that it remains a dynamic and relevant resource.

Protection and secrecy: Consider adding protective elements, such as symbols or spells, to keep the energy within your Book of Shadows sacred. Store it in a safe and private place.

Make it yours: Your Book of Shadows is a reflection of your own spiritual journey. Let it evolve and adapt as you grow in your magical practice.

Remember, there are no strict rules, so let your intuition guide you. Your Book of Shadows serves as a personal and sacred tool, designed to document your spiritual evolution. Seize this auspicious time of rebirth and renewal to inscribe your intentions, spells and reflections, taking note throughout the book of the topics that most interest you. During the Winter Solstice and the dawn of the new year you stand at the threshold of your spiritual journey, so let your curiosity guide you. Explore and research your topics of interest, and enrich your Book of Shadows with each new-found insight.

Ideas to Include in Your Book of Shadows

- **Elemental balance**: Consider each element (earth, air, fire, water and spirit) and how they currently manifest in your life. Did you want to move house just to be closer to the water? Perhaps you like to light candles and become easily transfixed by the flame? Think about which elements you are most drawn to and how they make you feel. Elements serve as building blocks of energies, and understanding their symbolic significance is key to enhancing your practice.

- **Dream exploration**: Delve into the meanings and messages behind your dreams, helping you to decode symbols and gain insights.

- **Moon phases**: Dedicate a spread of your Book of Shadows to each moon phase, exploring its energy and how it influences different aspects of your life.

- **Herbology**: Focus on the magical properties of herbs, exploring their uses, correspondences and how to incorporate them into your practice.

- **Wheel of the Year**: The Wheel of the Year is a cyclical calendar used in many pagan and Wiccan traditions, marking the changing seasons and celebrating eight key festivals, also known as Sabbats. These festivals include the solstices, equinoxes, and cross-quarter days, each representing different aspects of nature's cycle. Draw the Wheel of the Year and its eight Sabbats, examining the themes, energies and rituals associated with each.

- **Crystal connection**: Explore the energies of different crystals and how they can be used for healing, protection or manifestation.

- **Rituals and ceremonies**: Outline step-by-step guides for specific rituals or ceremonies that are important to your path.

3

Feasting and Winter Wishes

I mmerse yourself in the comforting warmth of hearth and home as we embark on a journey through the enchanting traditions of feasting and winter wishes. In this chapter we explore the timeless rituals of gathering with loved ones, crafting meaningful gifts and savouring the flavours of the season. From ancient roots to modern tables, we uncover the culinary delights of Yule, blending old-world recipes with contemporary twists. Join me as we delve into the magic of the kitchen, revealing the secrets of kitchen witchery and learning about different tools, herbs and spices to infuse your cooking with intention. So gather round the table, ignite the flames of kinship and let the magic fill your stomach and heart.

Connecting with Community

Yule is a festival that sees families and communities united in commemorating the year's end and honouring the souls of departed friends and family. Transcending personal beliefs, this time of year highlights the significance of shared customs and treasured traditions that have been passed down through the generations. From merry drinking, feasting and singing to honouring gods and ancestral spirits by means of rituals, it's a time of fostering community magic and connecting with those closest to us.

Conscious Crafting and Magical Gifting

Contrary to popular belief, the act of giving presents isn't a scheme cooked up by capitalism. It has deep historical roots, which can be traced back to ancient traditions such as Saturnalia, an ancient Roman festival held in honour of the god Saturn; as well as *Dies Natalis Solis Invicti*, which was a celebration of the birth of the Roman god Sol, or the sun, celebrated on 25 December. When Christianity gained traction in Rome, gift-giving was once again reimagined and became symbolic of the offerings that were brought to Jesus by the Three Wise Men. In pagan times, gifts were often exchanged as a symbol of goodwill and prosperity for the coming year. The exchange of gifts was also a way to honour the gods and ask for their favour and protection. People would be crafty and resourceful, traditionally making use of available materials and natural elements to craft toys, decorations, weapons, clothes and tools to gift, in order to forge bonds and showcase loyalty to their family and community. Later these pagan traditions gave birth to 'gift wakes' in the northern part of the world, where communities would gather in the spirit of making gifts together and listening to the master of the house read stories.

One enchanting handmade gift suggestion for Yule is a wish *tonttu*. Made using only a few simple items, this tiny, enchanting gnome-doll transforms wishes into promises for the approaching year. Why not introduce a heart-warming new tradition this year? Craft a wish *tonttu* for each member of your family and gather round the Yule tree or by the hearth on the eve of the Winter Solstice. Then share your hopes for the coming year – you can place written messages with your *tonttus* for the night, or you may prefer to whisper them to these magical creatures. As the Yule festivities unfold, these enchanting beings work their subtle magic, transforming into tokens of manifestation. Come morning, with the rising sun of Yule day, the *tonttus* return to their owners, now carrying the essence of good fortune and the hope that the recipient's desires will come to fruition the following year.

The wish *tonttu* can serve as a delightful decoration or a thoughtful handmade offering during the festive season. Below are instructions on crafting your own Yule wish *tonttu*; remember to personalize it by adjusting the colours and details to your liking!

> *If the modern frenzy of Christmas shopping feels disconnected from the genuine spirit of giving, consider a more deliberate approach to it this year. Crafting your own Yule presents not only connects you to ancestral practices, but also enables you to infuse each gift with heartfelt intention and well-wishes. Elevate a handmade gift by including a letter or message explaining the intention woven into the present – after all, during this season of giving, the sentiment truly matters.*

Yule Wish Tonttu

Materials needed:

1. Wine-bottle cork
2. Wooden ball for the head (the same width as, or bigger than, your cork)
3. PVA glue
4. Scissors
5. Paper
6. Red felt fabric for the hat and outfit
7. Cotton or faux fur for the beard
8. Black Sharpie or other pen

Instructions:

Step 1: Prepare the Wine-Bottle Cork and Wooden Ball

Ensure the wine-bottle cork and wooden ball are clean and dry.

Step 2: Prepare the Figurine

Glue your wooden ball onto the top of your cork. Let this dry at least for a few hours.

Step 3: Make the Hat

Cut the hat shape out of felt, as shown here. Roll the felt into a cone shape until it fits the size of your wooden ball  and glue the edges to secure it. The size of your felt cutout will vary, depending on the size of your *tonttu*'s head. I recommend cutting out a larger shape, as you can roll the felt tighter for a smaller fit. Once fully dried, glue the hat onto the *tonttu*'s head.

Step 4: Design the Outfit

Cut the cloak out of felt, as shown here. I recommend cutting out a paper stencil

first to get the measurements right for your unique cork. Start off with a larger shape, as you can always trim this down to the perfect size and shape. Once you have cut your shape using felt, roll it into a cone, with a smaller opening at the top and a large opening at the bottom. Do a few practice runs wrapping the cloak around the cork before securing it with glue.

Step 5: Add a Beard and Facial Features

Cut a small piece of cotton or faux fur to create the *tonttu*'s beard. Glue it to the middle of your wooden ball, before adding in eyes and a nose above the beard with a Sharpie or other pen.

Step 6: Allow to Dry

Ensure all the glued components are secure, then allow your *tonttu* to dry completely before handling or gifting it.

> *Decorate your gift parcels with unique gift stamps made using raw potatoes. Cut a large potato in half, press a small cookie-cutter of your choice through the potato and carve around the edges with a small sharp knife, removing any potato around the shape. Wipe off any excess moisture from the potato, brush it with paint and stamp away! When you're done, just leave the potato stamp in some cold water, where it will stay fresh for a few days. If left to dry, the potato will shrink and the surface of the stamp will become uneven.*

From Ancient Roots to Modern Tables

The Yule feast was the highlight of Nordic pagan celebrations, a time when everyone gathered to celebrate the end of winter's harshness and the arrival of longer days. At the heart of this grand affair was the sacrificial *blót*, a sacred ritual in which farm animals – symbols of prosperity – were offered in homage to the many different gods of the pagans. The animals were displayed outside homes and their blood was sprinkled on altars, people and walls, using enchanted magical twigs. The sacrificial bounty was then prepared over the hearth fire and shared in a huge feast.

Alongside the meat and the Yule ham, a wide variety of other dishes would be served, including fish, porridge and bread. As everyone ate and drank their mead, cups were raised in honour of Odin for victory and power, Njördr and Freya for peace and bountiful seasons, as well as to departed kin and ancestors. During the celebration, people made promises called Yule oaths. Declarations uttered under the sacred blanket of the solstice sky, these were considered binding and unbreakable by ancient pagan law. While anything could be promised, breaking a Yule oath could have serious consequences – in some cases resulting in the person's death. Perhaps this was a precursor of the modern-day New Year's resolution, where we vow to better ourselves and make positive changes in the coming year.

Modern Nordic Christmas feasts showcase a delightful blend of both traditional and contemporary culinary delicacies, paying homage to the ancient Yule feast while incorporating more modern preferences. At the heart of modern Nordic Christmas mornings sits a cherished tradition: rice porridge. This humble dish, known as *risengrynsgrøt* in Norway or as *joulupuuro* in Finland, traces its origins to the ancient Nordic Yule feast. Once a symbolic offering to appease ancestral spirits and gods, this creamy rice porridge is now generously sprinkled with sugar and cinnamon and symbolizes warmth, family and the coming together of loved ones. The tradition of hiding a 'good-fortune almond' in the porridge echoes the age-old customs of hiding tokens or prizes during the Yule celebrations.

As the day progresses, another beloved feature of modern Nordic Christmas tables emerges: *glögi*. This mulled wine, infused with aromatic spices such as cloves and cinnamon and often served with almonds and raisins mixed in, traces its roots to the ancient Nordic penchant for warm spiced drinks during the Winter Solstice. *Glögi*, reminiscent of the mead or ale shared long ago, serves as a soul-warming cosy drink, often enjoyed with a shot of vodka to make the festivities extra-merry.

FEASTING AND WINTER WISHES

Traditional Glögi Recipe

Ingredients:

- 170 ml water
- 85 g caster sugar
- 1–2 cinnamon sticks
- 10 whole cloves
- 1 tsp cardamom seeds
- 1 piece of fresh ginger
- 100 ml blackcurrant cordial (I like to use Belvoir Farm Natural Blackcurrant Cordial)
- 0.75 litres red wine / non-alcoholic red wine
- raisins
- almonds (peeled or flaked)
- vodka (optional)

Instructions:

1. Bring to a simmer 100 ml of water, the sugar and spices for 15 minutes. Strain the spiced liquid and add it back into the pan.

2. Mix in the blackcurrant cordial and wine (opt for an alcohol-free wine if preferred). Add the remaining 70 ml of water.

3. Heat the mixture, but do not bring to a boil.

4. Sprinkle the raisins and almonds into the glasses.

5. Pour the traditional *glögi* into glasses or mugs and, if desired, spike the drink with vodka.

In most Finnish homes, *glögi* finds delightful companionship with *joulutorttus*, traditional Finnish Christmas pastries (the name translates as 'Christmas tart'). These flaky Christmas tarts boast a sweet prune- or plum-jam filling peeking through their folded corners and are not just a treat for the tastebuds, but also a visual delight, resembling a star or pinwheel.

Joulutorttu Recipe

Ingredients:

- 1 sheet puff pastry (store-bought or home-made; I like using Jus-Rol ready rolled puff-pastry sheets)

- prune or plum jam (feel free to substitute any other jam or preserve of your liking; as *traditional prune jam can be tricky to find, you can make your own: see below).*

- *1 egg for the egg wash*
- *icing sugar for dusting*

Prune-jam ingredients:

- *250 g dried prunes*
- *sugar or cinnamon, to taste*

Instructions:

Prune jam:

1. In a saucepan, cover the prunes with water and bring to the boil. Lower the heat to medium, stirring regularly.

2. Once the prunes start to soften, you can begin mashing them, until you reach a thick, jammy consistency. Add more water, if needed. You may wish to add some sugar for extra sweetness, or cinnamon for flavour.

3. The home-made jam should be stored in an airtight container and kept in the fridge, where it will last for up to one week.

Joulutorttu:

1. Preheat the oven to 200°C on a fan setting.

2. Roll out the puff-pastry sheet until you reach a thickness of about 0.5 cm. Measure your pastry sheet and divide it roughly into an equal number of squares. I recommend 8 x 8 cm squares, but feel free to make them smaller or bigger, based on the size of your sheet and the number of pastries you want to make.

3. Cut an incision, approximately half of the length to the centre of the square, in every corner.

4. Next, fold every other corner into the centre of the square and press down, before placing a generous dollop of jam into the centre of the tart.

5. Place the prepared pastries on a baking sheet lined with parchment paper and brush them with an egg wash.

6. Bake in the preheated oven for about 10–13 minutes or until the pastries turn golden brown and puffy.

7. Allow them to cool before dusting them with icing sugar and serving them alongside a warm cup of *glögi* for a cosy Christmas treat.

Modern-day Yule feasts are about far more than just porridge and cosy warm drinks. Much like their ancestors, modern Nordic families embrace a spread that celebrates the bounty of the season. Roasted meats (particularly ham), often accompanied by gravlax (cured salmon), echo the sacrificial offerings of the past. Root vegetables such as potatoes, carrots and swedes, cooked in various ways and often served in the form of casseroles, are a celebration of the plentiful autumn harvest. Additionally, the table often boasts an array of pickled herring – homage to the significance of fish in ancient Nordic diets – as well as home-made cheeses and various different jams and condiments, stewed from preserved summer and autumn berries.

Another important element that has sustained Nordic folk for centuries and that often occupies a place of honour in the middle of the Christmas dinner table is *joululimppu* (which translates as 'Christmas loaf'), a dark, sweet bread typically made from rye, wheat, malt or wort and flavoured with ingredients such as fennel and bitter orange. *Joululimppu* holds significant cultural importance in Finnish and

Swedish Christmas food traditions: after taking the bread out of the oven, previous generations would often put a log in its place, to ward off poverty. To ensure a good rye harvest for the upcoming year, the home would be adorned with *himmelis* (see page 59), and people could even prophesy the next year's crop by throwing straw up into the ceiling and watching the stems fall in different patterns.

*

Let this year be a year of forging new and heartfelt traditions – gather your loved ones to take part in a heartfelt winter Wish Bread-making ritual. On the eve of the solstice, gather straw, herbs such as juniper, rosemary and pine, and spices such as cinnamon sticks and cloves, and arrange them around a flickering candle. In the candlelight, prepare a bread dough and, as the sun begins to set, blow out the candle with a blessing and leave the dough to rise throughout the solstice night.

As the first rays of dawn paint the solstice-day sky, gather the family to shape the bread together. Unite in the shared task of pulling small dough balls, embedding each with crushed cardamom, raisins, dried fruit and nuts. With the shaping of each dough ball, weave wishes for another person, speaking them aloud, sharing heartfelt desires that might reveal unexpected insights and understanding among family members.

While the wish-filled bread bakes in the oven, set the table, adorned with the remnants of your evening candle altar – straw, herbs and spices. Ready your hearts and appetites for the bounty of the Wish Bread and give gratitude for the special people in your life.

Wish Bread Recipe

Ingredients:

- 2 sachets of dry yeast (14 g)
- 500 ml lukewarm water
- 1 tsp sugar
- 800 g strong bread flour (I like using both white and wholewheat mixed together; you can adjust the ratios to taste, or use one or the other), plus some extra for dusting
- 2 tsp salt
- Seeds, nuts, herbs and spices (you can add these into your bread dough according to your taste or intention; feel free to get creative!)

Instructions:

1. First, activate your yeast by mixing it into the water with the sugar. Leave for 5-10 minutes, until the surface is bubbly.

2. In a separate bowl, mix your dry ingredients.

3. Create a well in the middle of your flour mixture and start pouring in the yeast water. You'll want to do this bit by bit, mixing it into the flour with a fork or spatula.

4. Once the dough starts to thicken, you can start kneading it with your hands.

5. After all the liquid has been incorporated, pour the dough onto a clean surface dusted with flour and knead until you have an elastic dough. A good way to test this is to roll it into a smooth ball and poke it – if the dough bounces back with ease, it's done.

6. Place the dough back into the bowl (you may want to use oil or flour at the base to stop it from sticking to the sides) and cover it with a tea towel. Leave to rest somewhere warm until the dough has doubled in size.

7. Preheat the oven to 200°C on a fan setting. I like to place a tray of boiling water at the bottom of the oven, as this helps the crust to form.

8. Shape your dough into bread rolls and place them onto a lined baking tray.

9. Bake in the oven for 25–30 minutes. The bread should sound hollow when you tap the base!

10. Leave to cool.

Yuletide Gift Basket

Hampers often serve as great Christmas gifts, but there are so many store-bought options they can sometimes lack a personal touch and practicality. Why not transform the typical cheese-and-crackers hamper into a truly magical Yuletide Gift Basket, where each item has a purpose and every element is thoughtfully selected?

Imagine this: nestled inside a classic wicker basket (handy if you need to carry chopped firewood), you'll find hand-knitted mittens, home-made gingerbread and hand-dipped taper candles, all lovingly wrapped in charming tea towels or cloth placemats, or elegantly laid atop a decorative tablecloth – providing an additional practical element to the gift, as well as acting as a sustainable option to replace single-use wrapping paper.

Enhancing this enchanting hamper is a bottle of *glögi*, carefully crafted following our earlier recipe and decorated with satin ribbon and a personalized label. Taking centre stage is a time-honoured handwritten recipe for my grandmother's traditional cognac mustard, perfect for glazing the centrepiece of your Yule feast: the ham. You may even have gone the extra mile and made the mustard yourself, finishing the basket with decorative berries and evergreens for some colour and a fresh scent: choose juniper for protection, pine for resilience and holly for hope, each element adding symbolic depth to your Yuletide Gift Basket. You can rest assured that this intentional hamper will bring warmth and the spirit of Yule to anyone fortunate enough to receive it.

Grandmother's Cognac Mustard Recipe

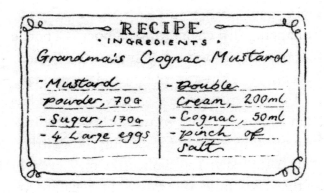

Ingredients:

- 70 g mustard powder
- 170 g sugar
- 4 medium / large eggs
- 200 ml double cream
- 50 ml cognac
- pinch of salt

Instructions:

1. In a bowl, mix the mustard powder and sugar together.

2. Add the eggs, double cream, cognac and pinch of salt to the mixture.

3. Place the mixture on top of a bain-marie (if you don't have a bain-marie, you can easily create your own: fill a pan with water and bring it to the boil, then place a smaller heatproof container, such as a metal bowl, inside the pan, ensuring that the bottom of the top container doesn't touch the water's surface).

4. Continually stir the mixture using a small whisk or spoon until the first bubble boils. In a bain-marie this should take about 15–20 minutes. Remove from the heat and allow to cool.

5. Store the mustard in a sterilized jar in the refrigerator for up to two weeks.

Magic in the Kitchen

Kitchen witchery is a practice that involves the use of herbs, spices and other ingredients to create magic in the kitchen. Each element carries specific magical properties, and the kitchen becomes a space for crafting spells and rituals through the selection and combination of these components. With practitioners often wishing to align their magic with the cycles of nature, kitchen witchery emphasizes the use of seasonal and locally sourced ingredients to celebrate the abundance of each season. Everyday kitchen tools, from a cup to a spoon, are seen as magical instruments and are considered an extension of magical will. For example, infusing your morning coffee with cinnamon and honey, while stirring clockwise to draw in warmth and energy, can invoke a day filled with comfort, sweetness and vitality. Kitchen witchery is one of the easiest ways to add intention and mindfulness into your everyday life. Many kitchen witches also draw inspiration from the culinary traditions of their ancestors and local folklore, for added depth and meaning to their practice.

It is important, in any nature-based spiritual or magical practice, for us to feel connected with the Earth and its elements, including the foods and ingredients that sustain us. The modern-day convenience of imported food reduces our reliance on seasonal, locally sourced produce, creating a disconnect between people and their natural environments. In many regions, including the northern part of the world, winter marks the end of the growing season. Winter cooking very quickly became an art of turning humble stored ingredients, often preserved in the late-summer months, into nourishing meals to feed communities. Few culinary creations embody the spirit of winter quite like hearty soups and stews – these comforting concoctions not only taste great, but also nourish both the body and the spirit.

A Witch's Enchantment Soup can easily be customized with any spell, herb or intention to transform a bowl of soup into a magical elixir. Kitchen witches trust their intuition in the kitchen and many do not follow strict recipes. Allow your instincts to guide the cooking process, and modify the recipe to your liking. Before doing so, however, take a look at some of the ways in which you might want to incorporate kitchen witchery into your cooking steps.

Before you begin your cooking process, select the intentions that you wish to infuse your Witch's Enchantment Soup with. It might help you to think about what you want to achieve from cooking this soup, or how you want the person eating it to feel. Are you perhaps making the soup for an important occasion, a celebration, a job interview or to help heal a physical ailment? To fully align with your intentions, write down what type of abundance you hope the soup will deliver. Choose herbs and spices from the suggestions below for flavour, and to infuse their corresponding properties into the soup.

FEASTING AND WINTER WISHES

- **Protection**: Basil, rosemary, cinnamon, garlic, sage, pepper, peppermint
- **Happiness**: Lavender, lemon balm, mint, feverfew
- **Insight**: Bay leaves, mugwort, thyme, lemongrass
- **Money**: Basil, cinnamon, patchouli, dill
- **Health**: Ginger, thyme, allspice, coriander
- **Wisdom**: Rosemary, sage, mint, chamomile, parsley, marjoram, thyme, cumin
- **Success**: Bay leaves, cinnamon, allspice, saffron, marjoram
- **Travel**: Juniper, basil, mint, caraway, dill, fennel, mustard, parsley
- **Peace**: Lavender, chamomile, rosemary, lemon balm
- **Love**: Rose, vanilla, coriander
- **Courage**: Cedar, mugwort, basil, pepper, chives, horseradish, nettle
- **Fertility**: Basil, red clover, rosemary, mint, cinnamon, coriander

Herbs and spices can be extremely powerful, not only adding flavour but also contributing potential health benefits. While many of these ingredients are commonly used in cooking and are generally considered safe for consumption, it's important to be aware of the safe quantities to eat, especially if you have any allergies, sensitivities or pre-existing medical conditions. If you experience any adverse reactions after consuming these ingredients, please discontinue their use and consult a healthcare professional.

Witch's Enchantment Soup Recipe

Ingredients:

- 1 kg carrots, peeled and thinly sliced
- 1 large potato, peeled and quartered
- water
- 50 g butter
- 1 large white onion, chopped
- 2 chicken or vegetable stock cubes

- 1 heaped tbsp honey
- 100 g feta or goat's cheese
- 400 g cream cheese
- pepper, to taste
- pinch of salt
- herbs and spices as required
- toppings (optional): roasted seeds, cream

Instructions:

1. In a pot, combine the sliced carrots and quartered potatoes. Add water until it's a few centimetres above the vegetables. Bring to the boil, then reduce the heat to a simmer until the vegetables are soft.

2. In a separate frying pan, melt the butter and fry the chopped onions on a low heat until caramelized. Set aside.

3. Once the vegetables are cooked, add the caramelized onions, stock cubes, honey, feta or goat's cheese, cream cheese, pepper and salt and any herbs or spices for their magical properties. Customize your choices to achieve the desired effect.

4. Remove the pot from the heat. Blend the mixture using an immersion blender until completely smooth. *Important*: remove the pot from the heat before blending, to avoid splattering.

5. Serve the enchanted soup hot, garnished with roasted seeds or a drizzle of cream for extra nourishment – enjoy!

While you peel your vegetables, imagine that you are removing any obstacles in the way of your intentions coming true. Carve sigils, runes or symbols into your potatoes and carrots before chopping them, visualizing each chopping motion as a way to seal the intentions into the vegetables. You can do the same for the butter, before melting this in your pan. When adding each ingredient, whisper your intentions for the soup, and remember that spoken spells do not have to rhyme or be particularly beautiful in order for them to work. As you bring your water to the boil, visualize it absorbing your intentions. For added potency, consider using moon-charged or crystal-charged water (see page 171).

The act of stirring your soup also becomes a ritual. Stirring clockwise is considered to invite in energies, whereas stirring anticlockwise is thought to banish energies. In this case, you definitely want to stir clockwise to amplify your desires. And consider what tool you wish to mix your soup with. Wooden utensils are associated with nature, grounding and growth, and stirring your soup with one of these can infuse it with earthy and stabilizing energies. If, however, you want to amplify the soup's transformative power or gain extra clarity on your intentions, consider using a metal utensil, as it charges whatever it touches with purity and balance. Glass utensils are a neutral material, allowing the true essence of your ingredients and your chosen intentions to shine, whereas stone or marble utensils amplify intentions of stability, strength and endurance.

Whichever utensil you choose, always remember that your powers are stronger than any materials. While selecting the right tool for your craft is beneficial, its effectiveness is always magnified when coupled with clear intent. Enjoy the enchanting journey of crafting each spoonful of your soup and remember to unleash your creativity in the process. There are no rights or wrongs in the magical world of kitchen witchery.

Yuletide Divination

For millennia, divination techniques have fascinated people all over the world. Although the first-known use of the word 'divination' was in the fourteenth century, divination has been practised in various forms throughout history, across different cultures and religions. One of the earliest recorded instances of divination practices, found in ancient China, dates from around 3000 BC, when ox shoulderblade bones and turtle shells were used to connect with ancestors and deities. Other early forms of divination include astrology (the interpretation of celestial bodies), which originated in Babylon, and lithomancy (the use of stones to predict the future), which was considered particularly popular among the ancient Greeks.

As civilizations evolved, so did divination, and medieval and Renaissance Europe saw the rise of astrology and tarot-readings – with many kings and queens, such as Elizabeth I and Catherine de' Medici, having their own astrologers. In contemporary times divination takes diverse forms, with modern practitioners including witches, pagans, neo-pagans and spiritualists, among those from many other backgrounds. Divination is now something that anyone can practise, and it is commonly accepted as a profound and deeply impactful tool – not only to seek insights into specific situations or questions, but also for self-reflection and personal growth. During the Yule season the age-old tradition of divination continues to hold significance for pagans and others alike, offering seekers the opportunity to gain clarity and wisdom as they illuminate their path into the new year.

Journey with Tarot

While it does not feature among the most traditional Nordic pagan tools, tarot is a deeply meaningful tool in any spiritual practice and can be extremely useful in helping to turn your gaze inwards during the Winter Solstice. Although they have become removed from the concept of 'fortune-telling', tarot cards can offer invaluable guidance in navigating life's twists and turns, helping to enrich self-care rituals and unveil glimpses of what energies may lie ahead. Originating in fifteenth-century Europe, tarot was initially a card game before transforming into a divination tool in the sixteenth and seventeenth centuries. At first these highly illustrated cards, commissioned by the rich to depict family and friends, were a luxury available only to a select few, before the era of the printing press. However, over time they evolved in their purpose from simple playing cards to divination tools, inviting people to navigate life's never-ending complexities.

The Minor Arcana

The seventy-eight cards of a traditional tarot deck are divided into two categories, known as the Major and Minor Arcana cards. The Minor Arcana cards comprise four suits, much like traditional playing cards: Wands (or staves), Cups, Swords and Pentacles (or coins), each associated with distinct aspects of life. Each suit also has different elemental, directional and astrological correspondences, further broadening the reader's interpretation of the cards. Below are just a few of the different correspondences and associated life aspects for each Minor Arcana suit.

Minor Arcana suit	Associated life aspects	Element	Season	Direction	Astrological signs
Wands	Creativity, passion, inspiration, ambition, adventure, energy, growth	Fire	Spring	South	Aries, Leo, Sagittarius
Cups	Emotions, relationships, intuition, creativity, compassion, inner reflection, matters of the heart	Water	Summer	West	Cancer, Scorpio, Pisces

Swords	Intellect, thoughts, challenges, clarity, communication, decision-making	Air	Autumn	East	Gemini, Libra, Aquarius
Pentacles	Material world, finances, stability, health, work, career, practicality, prosperity	Earth	Winter	North	Taurus, Virgo, Capricorn

As well as being of a certain suit, each Minor Arcana is numbered from Ace through to Ten, followed by the Court Cards (Page, Knight, Queen and King). The numbers offer a narrative that reflects a progression or evolution of the themes represented by the suit. In other words, the numbers can offer insights into what stage someone is at in their journey within their respective suit and associated life aspects. Here is a breakdown of the significance of numbering in the Minor Arcana.

✦ **Aces (1):** Symbolize new beginnings, potential and the essence of the suit's energy. Aces signify the spark or seed of the suit's theme, representing opportunities in the area of life related to the suit.

- **Twos (2):** Often depict duality, balance or partnerships within the suit's theme. Twos can represent choices, relationships or the initial stages of cooperation and harmony.

- **Threes (3):** Reflect expansion, growth and collaboration within the suit. Threes signify progress, development or the manifestation of ideas initiated in the preceding cards.

- **Fours (4):** Symbolize stability, foundation and structure within the suit's theme. Fours represent a solidification or establishment of the suit's elements.

- **Fives (5):** Typically portray conflict, challenges, or disruptions within the suit's realm. Fives indicate changes, adjustments or conflicts that might disrupt the balance established earlier.

- **Sixes (6):** Represent harmony, balance and resolution after the conflicts depicted in the Fives. Sixes often signify reconciliation, healing or finding solutions.

- **Sevens (7):** Symbolize assessment, evaluation or a moment of reflection within the suit. They can indicate a need for revaluation or appraisal before progressing further.

- **Eights (8):** Signify progress, movement or advancement within the suit's realm. Eights represent momentum, growth or overcoming obstacles.

- **Nines (9):** Symbolize approaching the end of a cycle and the fulfillment or attainment that is almost within reach. Nines often represent the final push and the last effort ended to achieve completion within the suit's theme.

- **Tens (10):** Represent completion, fulfilment or the end of a cycle within the suit's narrative. Tens signify the culmination of the suit's energies, wrapping up the storyline initiated by the Aces.

The Court Cards (Page, Knight, Queen, King) represent personalities or individuals and do not follow a numbered sequence. From the eager and curious Page to the mature and authoritative King, they embody different aspects and stages of maturity within the suit's theme. Here is how the Court Cards are typically interpreted.

- **Pages:** Represent youthful energy, curiosity and a learning phase. They signify new beginnings, messages or the initial stages of exploration within the suit's realm. Pages can indicate a person or situation that embodies these qualities or that brings messages related to the suit's theme.

- **Knights:** Symbolize action, energy and movement. They represent progression, drive or the pursuit of goals within the suit. Knights embody the qualities of enthusiasm, ambition and a willingness to embark on quests or adventures related to the suit's element.

- **Queens:** Portray nurturing, receptivity and maturity. They symbolize emotional depth, intuition and wisdom within the suit's realm. Queens represent individuals or aspects of yourself that embody qualities of empathy, understanding and emotional stability.

- **Kings:** Represent authority, leadership and mastery. They embody the pinnacle of maturity and wisdom within the suit's theme. Kings symbolize individuals or aspects that are characterized by strength, mastery and a solid command of the suit's energy.

The Major Arcana

The Major Arcana consists of twenty-two unique cards, each of which is symbolic with powerful archetypical pictures and themes. These cards often depict major life events and experiences, spiritual lessons and fundamental influences. If the Minor Arcana cards are the individual pages of a book elaborating on the day-to-day aspects of life, the Major Arcana cards make up the main chapters of the book, each holding within it profound life lessons, which are often thought to be more fated than the messages of their Minor Arcana counterparts. The Major Arcana is thought to tell the story of the 'Fool's journey', with the Fool being the first card of the Major Arcana. This metaphorical voyage is one of self-discovery, growth and transformation, where the Fool goes through cyclical trials and tribulations before reaching the final Major Arcana card – 'the World' – and gaining new-found wisdom and spiritual enlightenment. Here is an overview of the Fool's journey through the Major Arcana.

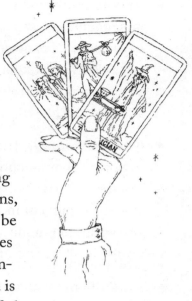

- **The Fool (0):** The beginning of the journey, depicting innocence, spontaneity and new beginnings. Upright, the Fool represents a soul embarking on a new adventure, unburdened by past experiences. Reversed (upside-down), the card suggests caution, hesitation or a reluctance to take risks, signalling a need for careful consideration and the avoidance of impulsive actions.

- **The Magician (I):** The Fool encounters the Magician, symbolizing harnessing personal power and manifestation. Upright, it signifies potential and action; reversed, it can imply manipulation or missed opportunities.

- **The High Priestess (II):** Here, the Fool encounters intuition and the mysteries of the subconscious. Upright, it signifies inner wisdom; reversed, it may indicate hidden agendas or secrets.

- **The Empress (III):** Representing nurturing and abundance, the Empress embodies creativity and growth. Upright, it signifies fertility and creation; reversed, it can suggest stagnation or neglect.

- **The Emperor (IV):** Depicts the encounter with structure and authority. Upright, it symbolizes stability and leadership; reversed, it may indicate authoritarianism or a lack of control.

- **The Hierophant (V):** Reflecting tradition and spiritual guidance, the Hierophant signifies conformity and teachings. Upright, it implies guidance; reversed, it can suggest rebellion or nonconformity.

- **The Lovers (VI):** This stage represents choices, relationships and harmony. Upright, the Lovers signifies partnerships; reversed, it may imply disharmony or unwise decisions.

- **The Chariot (VII):** Symbolizing control and determination, the Chariot represents willpower and direction. Upright, it signifies success; reversed, it may imply a lack of control or obstacles.

- **Strength (VIII):** Here, the Fool encounters inner strength and courage. Upright, it signifies fortitude and compassion; reversed, it can suggest inner doubts or weaknesses.

- **The Hermit (IX):** Symbolizing introspection and the seeking of wisdom, the Hermit embodies solitude and reflection. Upright, it signifies inner guidance; reversed, it may imply isolation or withdrawal.

- **Wheel of Fortune (X):** Representing life's cycles and fate, the Wheel of Fortune brings changes and is a reminder of destiny. Upright, it signifies turning points; reversed, it may imply setbacks or a resistance to letting things run their natural course.

- **Justice (XI):** Symbolizing balance and fairness, Justice represents accountability and ethical decisions. Upright, it signifies fairness and truth; reversed, it can suggest injustice or a lack of balance.

- **The Hanged Man (XII):** Signifying a shift in perspective and sacrifice, the Hanged Man embodies surrender and new outlooks. Upright, it represents surrender or suspension; reversed, it may imply impatience, a resistance to change or delays.

- **Death (XIII):** Representing transformation and endings, Death brings rebirth and closure. Upright, it signifies change and transformation; reversed, it can suggest resistance to change or stagnation.

- **Temperance (XIV):** Symbolizing balance and harmony, Temperance embodies moderation and patience. Upright, it signifies slow-moving energies and taking the middle path; reversed, it may hint at imbalances and the inability to adapt to new situations.

- **The Devil (XV):** Reflecting materialism, temptation and bondage, the Devil represents vices and limitations. Upright, it signifies addictive tendencies and unhealthy attachments; reversed, it can suggest liberation or breaking free from constraints.

- **The Tower (XVI):** Symbolizing sudden upheaval and revelations, the Tower brings the destruction of old beliefs or structures. Upright, it signifies sudden change, spiritual awakening or chaos; reversed, it may imply the fear of starting over or avoiding disaster.

- **The Star (XVII):** Signifying hope and inspiration, the Star represents guidance and healing. Upright, it signifies hope and faith; reversed, it can suggest a lack of faith or despair.

- **The Moon (XVIII):** Representing the subconscious and illusions, the Moon unveils hidden truths and fears. Upright, it signifies confusion or illusions where trusting your intuition is key; reversed, it implies the need for healing and shadow work (exploring and integrating suppressed or unconscious aspects of yourself) to gain more clarity.

- **The Sun (XIX):** Marking joy and clarity, the Sun brings positivity and vitality. Upright, it signifies joy and success; reversed, it can suggest temporary setbacks, lack of clarity or the need to do Inner Child Work (exploration of emotions and memories that you were forced to repress in childhood).

- **Judgement (XX):** Symbolizing awakening and transformation, Judgement represents reassessment and rebirth. Upright, it signifies renewal and accountability; reversed, it may imply self-doubt or a refusal to change.

- **The World (XXI):** The final stage, signifying completion and integration, the World marks the end of a cycle and the attainment of true spiritual wisdom. As the Fool reaches the World in his journey, he understands that every step along the way – no matter how seemingly random or chaotic – has contributed to his personal growth and enlightenment.

While it can be useful to study the meanings of the cards and other associated aspects, tarot-reading should be an intuitive process. It is important to understand that all the answers we seek exist innately within the deck, but also within us.

Your own interpretation is a window to your subconscious mind, where you are more connected to the universal energies around you. Learning to trust your intuition and instincts can sometimes be a much longer process than actually learning the meaning of each tarot card, but ultimately a much more important one.

There are a lot of misconceptions about tarot and tarot readers. Before you embark on your own personal journey with the cards it is important to understand that these myths are exactly that: myths. You may have heard that you should not buy your first tarot deck and that it needs to be gifted to you. This is believed to originate in a time when, in some places, it was a crime to use tarot cards, and you needed to know the right person in order to acquire your deck. Although these days receiving a tarot deck as a gift can be a special experience, it is not a requirement. Many practitioners purchase their own decks, and the connection with the cards often deepens when the deck is chosen based on personal resonance. The idea that a gifted deck is more powerful is baseless – your intention and your connection matter more than the method of acquisition. Choosing a deck that speaks to you and that aligns with your energy is an important part of building a meaningful connection with the cards.

To achieve a strong personal connection and an energetic link with your cards, take some time to introduce yourself to the deck. Hold the cards in your hands and express your intentions for using them. To get to know your unique deck of cards, you may even wish to ask questions like, 'What are your strengths?' or 'How can I best work with you?' and the cards drawn will offer insights into the deck's personality and strengths. You can also place the tarot deck under your pillow or near your bedside table when you sleep, which can facilitate a subtle energetic exchange while you rest. Alternatively, spend time meditating with the cards during your waking hours. Pull a single card each day and allow its imagery to guide your meditation. This practice not only connects you to your deck, but also deepens your understanding of the card's meanings.

Tarot cards are not fortune-telling tools; instead they offer insights into current energies and potential paths. The future is not set in stone, and tarot is more about guidance than prediction. This is why anyone can learn to read tarot cards. While some people may have a natural inclination, tarot-reading is a skill that can be developed through study, practice and an open mind. Psychic abilities can enhance a reading, but they are not a prerequisite. Tarot relies on intuition, which everyone possesses; and trusting your instincts, together with an established connection with the cards, is key. Tarot is not tied to any specific belief system and is a versatile tool used by people from various spiritual backgrounds, including those who do not adhere to any particular dogma.

One of the biggest misconceptions about tarot is that the cards hold evil powers or that reading them is 'fraternizing with the Devil'. Tarot cards themselves are neutral. It's the reader's intent and interpretation that matter the most. Tarot is a tool for self-reflection and guidance, not a source of malevolent forces. Once you connect with your own deck, you will quickly discover the cards' illuminating nature, providing comfort and valuable perspective.

In addition to the aforementioned tips to connect with your deck, it is always a good idea to keep a tarot journal in which you document your daily draws, impressions and feelings about the cards. This helps you track your progress and understand the nuances of the deck, gaining insight over time. Remember that building a connection with your tarot deck is a personal journey; be patient, open-minded and allow the relationship to unfold naturally over time. Create simple rituals around your tarot practice, such as lighting a candle, doing a meditation or creating a sacred space before doing a reading. As you spend more time with your deck, you'll probably find that the cards become a familiar and trusted companion.

Before each reading, cleanse your tarot deck to remove any residual energies. You will often see people knocking on their deck with their knuckles or tapping the deck on the table before starting to shuffle it. This is probably one of the most common ways to cleanse the deck with the power of your intention. You can, however, also opt to place your deck in moonlight, sunlight or near a cleansing crystal, such as clear quartz. I like to use a smudging tool or a sound-bowl, which cleanses using the vibrational properties of sound; but my favourite way to cleanse is by using a hawthorn wand, which I run over the cards, before tapping on all four sides of the deck to represent the four cardinal directions.

As you begin your reading, start visualizing your question or intention. Take a few deep breaths to calm your mind and centre your focus. Clearly articulate the question you want guidance on, and be as specific and direct in your wording as possible. Pose your question either aloud or silently and, when you feel ready, begin to shuffle your tarot deck. Shuffling – much like everything else in tarot – should be personal to you. Some people choose to 'cut' the deck, dividing it into, typically, three separate piles, before intuitively combining them again and pulling the card at the top, although most people opt for a traditional loose shuffling technique. You may even wish to fan all the cards out on the table in front of you and run your hand over the top, feeling for differences in temperature or a tingling sensation as a sign of which card to draw.

The questions that you ask do not need to be specific to a person or situation; especially if you are reading for yourself, focus on seeking guidance as opposed to solutions. Some of my favourite questions to ask my tarot deck include: What do I need to know right now? Where am I lacking? What do I need to focus my energy on this month, or next season? How can I shift the reality of my mindset? What do I need to learn right now? And what should I be paying attention to, or be aware of?

Another great way to read tarot is by paying attention to the positioning of the cards in your deck. For example, when you are feeling stuck in life, grab your deck and find the Death card. Make note of the card behind it, as this is what you need to leave behind; and of the card in front of it, as this shows you what you should focus on instead. If you are looking for insight into a romantic relationship, find the Lovers in your deck. The card behind the Lovers signifies where the disconnect lies, while the card in front tells you where to find connection in your relationship.

Lastly, if you're feeling emotionally drained, shuffle and look for the Ace of Cups. The card behind represents things that are depleting your energy storages, while the card in front reveals how you can fill your cup back up.

Here are a few other ways in which you may wish to read your cards. Whether you are a beginner or a seasoned tarot reader, a Past, Present and Future spread is always a go-to.

Past, Present and Future Spread

Card positions:

- ✦ **Card 1 (left):** Past – represents the factors that have led to the current situation.

- ✦ **Card 2 (centre):** Present – reflects the current circumstances or challenges.

- ✦ **Card 3 (right):** Future – offers insights into potential outcomes or resolutions.

Probably the most well-known tarot spread is called a Celtic Cross, and, while it may look intimidating with its ten cards, when you are faced with a complex life situation this spread can provide a great deal of much-needed insight.

Celtic Cross Spread

Card positions:

+ **Card 1 (centre):** Present – the current situation.
+ **Card 2 (crossing card):** Challenge – what may hinder or help the situation.
+ **Card 3 (above):** Conscious Mind – your thoughts or attitudes.
+ **Card 4 (below):** Subconscious Mind – hidden influences or feelings.
+ **Card 5 (left):** Recent Past – events leading up to the present.
+ **Card 6 (right):** Near Future – upcoming influences.
+ **Card 7 (bottom right):** Your Attitude – your approach to the situation.
+ **Card 8 (above card 7):** External Influences – outside factors affecting the situation.
+ **Card 9 (above card 8):** Hopes and Fears – your desires or concerns.
+ **Card 10 (above card 9:** Final Outcome – the likely result of the situation.

In the spirit of the season, the Winter Solstice Wisdom Spread helps you to ground in the energy of the present, all the while looking ahead into the future with positivity and clarity.

Winter Wisdom Spread

Card positions:

- **Card 1 (centre):** The Present Energy – represents the current state or energy around you.
- **Card 2 (top):** Which obstacles or challenges to let go of and release during this season.
- **Card 3 (bottom):** Guidance on what to nurture or focus on for inner growth.
- **Card 4 (left):** How to invite more light, joy and positivity into your life.
- **Card 5 (right):** Insights into what intentions to plant for the upcoming season.

There are a few notable figures in Nordic mythology that emanate the same energy as some Major Arcana cards, so look out for these in your readings and ask yourself the corresponding questions.

- **The Fool – Loki, the Trickster:** The Fool represents the journey of discovery and unpredictability. In Norse mythology, Loki embodies the Trickster archetype, navigating the realms with mischievous charm. Both Loki and the Fool invite you to embrace the unknown and find wisdom in unexpected places. Ask yourself: How can I navigate the unpredictable aspects of my journey with curiosity and openness? But also: Am I being honest with myself about the authenticity of the path that I am on, or would a different path be more suited to me?

- **The Magician – Odin:** Both Odin and the Magician possess the power of manifestation and transformation. Odin's magical pursuits and the Magician's mastery of the elements underscore their shared theme of harnessing spiritual energies. Ask yourself: How can I tap into my inner power to manifest positive transformations in my life? What are my strengths and am I playing to them?

- **The High Priestess – Frigg, Queen of Asgard:** Both Frigg and the High Priestess embody feminine intuition and hidden wisdom. Frigg's silent influence over the fate of the world parallels the High Priestess's connection to the mysteries beyond the veil. Ask yourself: How can I deepen my connection to intuition and access hidden wisdom in my life? Am I in touch or out of touch with my divinity?

- **The Emperor – Thor, God of Thunder:** The Emperor's authority and strength find resonance in Thor. Both exude leadership and power, representing the disciplined force that brings order to chaos. Thor's protective nature mirrors the Emperor's role as a stabilizing force. Ask yourself: In what areas of my life can I embrace disciplined leadership and bring order to chaos? Am I willing to make a commitment and stand strong in the face of adversity when I find that my discipline is being challenged?

- **The Hierophant – Tyr, God of Law and Honour:** Tyr, upholder of law and honour, aligns with the Hierophant's archetype. Both symbolize adherence to spiritual principles and societal norms. Tyr's sacrifices for justice and the Hierophant's role as a spiritual guide emphasize their shared commitment to higher ideals. Ask yourself: How can I align my actions with spiritual principles and contribute to justice? How are my spiritual beliefs serving me and others?

- **The Lovers – Freyja and Freyr:** The Lovers card reflects the theme of sacred unions, choices and duality. In Norse mythology the sibling deities Freyja and Freyr embody the essence of love, fertility and choice. Their intertwined stories align with the Lovers' exploration of relationships and decisions. Ask yourself: Do I respect and accept both the dark and light parts of myself? What choices will I make about who I want to be in this lifetime and how I choose to connect with others?

- **The Chariot – *Skidbladnir*, Freyr's Magical Ship:** The Chariot's journey and triumph connect with *Skidbladnir*, Freyr's magical ship that travels across land, sea and sky. Crafted by skilled dwarves and renowned as the finest ship of all, *Skidbladnir* and the Chariot symbolize direction and triumph over challenges through focused determination and a sense of purpose. Ask yourself: What tools are in my toolbox to overcome difficult situations and challenges in my life? How can I steer my life with purpose?

- **Strength – Thor's Strength:** As well as corresponding to the Emperor, Thor's legendary strength resonates with the archetype of Strength in the tarot. Both represent not only physical might, but also the inner strength needed to overcome challenges with courage and compassion. Ask yourself: Am I willing to face my fears and address my trauma in pursuit of strength and resilience? Am I ready to find the power within me?

- **The Hermit – Mímir, the Wise Being:** Mímir, known for his wisdom and solitude, echoes the Hermit's archetype. Both embody a quest for inner knowledge through introspection and withdrawal from the external world. Ask yourself: In what ways can I embrace solitude and introspection to gain inner wisdom and clarity? Am I giving myself enough time and space to process things or am I simply charging forward and find myself repeating cycles?

- **The Wheel of Fortune – Norns, Weavers of Fate:** The Norns – female beings who create and control fate – are powerful entities in Nordic mythology that shape the course of human destinies, even surpassing gods in their influence. Norns align with the Wheel of Fortune; both emphasizing the cyclical nature of life, the interconnectedness of destinies and the ever-turning wheel of time. Ask yourself: Do I trust the universe to have my best interests at heart and accept that 'what goes around comes around'? Am I trying to force things and keep finding myself back where I started?

When you pull your cards, notice which way round they appear: are they upright or reversed? If you are reading for another person who is sitting in front of you, make sure you are consistent in which way round you are reading for them, so that you can pay attention to this detail. The meaning of a reversed tarot card can vary, depending on the card itself and its place in the spread. Some readers interpret reversed tarot cards as carrying the opposite meaning of the upright card, while others see them as carrying an intensified energy. Another way to read tarot-card reversals is to interpret them as delays or blockages on the seeker's path. However, there is no right or wrong way to read reversed tarot cards and it is always up to the reader's intuition, skill and experience to interpret the card within the wider context of the reading.

Whether reversed or upright, when you pull a card, notice what your first thought was when you saw it, and allow that to shape your interpretation process. Ask yourself: How did I feel when I first saw the card? Did another image, thought or perhaps even another card come to mind when I looked at it? Your initial reaction is often instinctive and unfiltered. It represents your intuition's immediate response to the symbolism, imagery and energy of the card, triggering a response from the deep recesses of your psyche and offering insights that might not be immediately apparent in logical or conscious analysis. The key is to learn how to trust your own intuition, ultimately shaping a practice that feels empowering, authentic and meaningful to you.

Casting Runes

Runes are ancient alphabets, characters or symbols that were used in various Germanic languages before the adoption of the Latin alphabet. The runic alphabets are called 'runic scripts' and they have historically been used by Germanic-speaking peoples, including the Vikings, for writing, divination and other magical purposes. There are several different runic alphabets, but the most well-known ones are the Elder Futhark, the Younger Futhark and the Anglo-Saxon Futhorc. The Elder Futhark, the oldest of the scripts, has twenty-four characters and was used by early Germanic tribes. The Younger Futhark, popular from the eighth to twelfth centuries, reduced the characters to sixteen and was predominantly used by the Norse people. Lastly, the Anglo-Saxon Futhorc, sometimes known as simply 'Futhorc', was used in England during the Anglo-Saxon period and was an extended version of the Elder Futhark, consisting of between twenty-six and thirty-three letters.

Runes have a lot of cultural and historical significance and have had various uses throughout time, including divination and runic readings, as well as inscribing objects such as weapons and memorial stones. Runes were, and still are, thought by many to possess magical properties and are used in rituals, spells and energy work. Much like tarot, runes offer insight into various aspects of life, with each rune carrying specific meanings, forming a symbolic language that remains relevant in modern practices, especially during the Yule season. According to Norse mythology, runes were bestowed as a gift by Odin and were used in various different practices during Yule, including as a way to mark the passing of the season. They were inscribed on various items, ranging from gifts and decorations to food, imbuing them with blessings and protective energies. Runic inscriptions have also been found on ancient drinking horns that would have been used to raise a toast to gods and heroes alike during Yuletide feasts.

The Elder Futhark

Rune	Transliteration	Meaning	Symbolism
ᚠ	Fehu	Cattle, wealth	Movable wealth, prosperity and success
ᚢ	Úruz	Aurochs, strength	Raw power, physical strength, courage
ᚦ	Turisaz	Thorn, giant	Chaos, defence, transformative power
ᚨ	Ansuz	God (Aesir)	Divine power, wisdom, communication
ᚱ	Raido	Ride, journey	Journeys (both physical and spiritual), change
ᚲ	Kaunan	Ulcer, torch	Knowledge, creativity, inspiration
ᚷ	Gebo	Gift	Generosity, partnerships, exchanges
ᚹ	Wunjo	Joy	Harmony, happiness, spiritual fulfilment
ᚺ	Hagalaz	Hail, air	Disruption, challenges, testing
ᚾ	Nauthiz	Need	Constraint, necessity, challenges
ᛁ	Isa	Ice	Stillness, patience, preservation
ᛃ	Jera	Year, harvest	Cycles, rewards
ᛇ	Eihwaz	Yew tree, tree of life	Endurance, transformation, stability
ᛈ	Perthro	Mysteries, secrets	Destiny, fate, divination

ᛉ	**Algiz**	Elk, protection	Connection with higher realms
ᛋ	**Sowilo**	Sun	Success, clarity, life energy
ᛏ	**Tiwaz**	Tyr, justice	Leadership, victory
ᛒ	**Berkano**	Birch tree, birth	New beginnings, growth, fertility
ᛖ	**Ehwaz**	Horse	Partnership, trust, progress
ᛗ	**Mannaz**	Man	Humanity, the self, psyche, awareness
ᛚ	**Laguz**	Water, lake	Intuition, emotions, healing
ᛜ	**Ingwaz**	Divine entity, Ing (Freyr)	Fertility, potential, internal growth, masculine energy
ᛞ	**Dagaz**	Day	Enlightenment, breakthrough, transformation
ᛟ	**Othala**	Ancestral property, heritage	Inheritance, ancestral wisdom, spiritual homeland

Rune sets are traditionally made with natural materials that are free and easily available, although you can choose whatever material you like. Popular choices include wood, stones, pebbles, bones and gemstones, and these can also make for a wonderful and unique gift to give during Yule. Reading runes involves casting them onto a surface (usually cloth) and interpreting those that land face-up. To interpret runes from a casting, it's essential to first familiarize yourself with the meanings of each rune. As you approach a casting, define a clear question or issue that you seek guidance on. Shuffle the runes and cast them, paying attention to specific positions within the casting. Observe patterns, clusters or the significance of individual rune placements. Consider both upright and reversed runes, for nuanced insights. Trust your intuition during the interpretation, holding space for your initial thoughts and expressions. Explore interactions and combinations between runes, and contextualize each rune within the overall reading. Document the runes and their interpretations for future reference and reflect on the insights that you've gained from the reading.

Scrying Mirrors

A scrying mirror, also known as a black mirror, is a divination tool used for scrying: a method of obtaining insights through gazing into reflective surfaces. Scrying – which originates from the Old English word *descry*, meaning 'to make out dimly' or 'to reveal or discover by careful observation or scrutiny' – took its earliest form in the shape of seeking answers and meaning on the reflective surface of water. The practice evolved over time into the use of crystal balls, mirrors and other objects. Traditionally, scrying mirrors were made from polished metals such as brass and copper, or by placing mercury or, more recently, aluminium foil, behind see-through glass. These days the mirrors are most often made from polished obsidian or blackened glass, although other dark and reflective materials are also used.

The primary purpose of a scrying mirror is to facilitate a trance-like state, allowing the scryer to perceive images, symbols or visions beyond the physical realm. Scrying mirrors are often employed to seek answers, receive guidance or connect with spiritual energies, with the reflective surface serving as a portal to the subconscious mind and, some believe, to the spiritual realm. The use of scrying mirrors dates back centuries and spans various cultures, with some historical references linking scrying mirrors to ancient civilizations such as the Egyptians and Greeks. However, their popularity surged during the Middle Ages and the Renaissance, as these eras saw a renewed interest in mysticism and occult practices. One of the most famous scryers in history was John Dee, a sixteenth-century mathematician, astronomer and advisor to Queen Elizabeth I. Dee used a crystal ball for scrying and documented his experiences in his diaries.

To create a scrying experience, choose a quiet and dimly lit space where you feel comfortable and won't be disturbed during your session. Relax through deep breathing or your own meditation practice, centring your energy and focusing on opening yourself up to receiving guidance and insights. Either hold your mirror or place it somewhere to stand at eye level, before gazing into the reflective surface. You want to tilt the mirror so that you do not see yourself in the reflection. Allow your mind to enter a trance-like state and be open to receiving impressions, images and messages. The key is not to focus too intensely. Pay attention to any symbols, images or visions that arise, and note any changes in colours or shadows within the mirror. Colours and shadows alongside any movement, or changes such as subtle shifts or distortions that catch your attention, can be symbolic or may represent different energies. Notice if there are any repeating patterns or motifs. These patterns may have personal significance or may convey information relevant to your current situation, but as always, above all else, trust your intuition. If you have a gut feeling or intuitive sense about something that you see or feel during the scrying session, take note of it. Intuition plays the most important part in divination practices.

Scrying mirrors are said to be most effective on dark nights, especially during the Winter Solstice, when the Norse believe the veil between worlds to be at its thinnest. This is a great time to practise rituals and carry out spiritual work that connects you to your ancestors. Talk to your living relatives about your family history or do some research yourself to find out more about your lineage. If you feel drawn to any particular individual, pay attention to this intuitive feeling and find out as much about them as you can. You may then wish to carry out a scrying session and attempt to tap into their energy. Talk to your mirror as if your ancestor is on the other side of it, using specific details about their life and addressing them by their name. Maintain an open heart and mind during this process, and trust that any emotions that arise are appropriate and related to your experience of contacting your ancestor. You can ask them questions or incorporate tarot or runes into your session, for an added layer of guidance and interpretation. If you don't have a specific person in mind, feel free to invite any ancestors to come forward. It can be helpful to hold items that may once have belonged to them, or incorporate any personal family items in the ritual. Here are some questions that you may wish to ask your ancestors:

What wisdom can you share? Ask your ancestors for guidance and wisdom that they have acquired through their life experiences. Seek advice on challenges that you may be facing or decisions that you need to make. This question invites ancestral insights that can help you navigate your present circumstances.

What family traditions should I honour? Enquire about family traditions, rituals or practices that hold significance for your ancestors. Learn about customs that were important to them and consider incorporating these into your own life. This question helps strengthen the connection to your ancestral roots and fosters a sense of continuity across generations.

How can I fulfil my life's purpose? Seek guidance on your life's purpose and mission. Ask your ancestors for insights into your unique path and the lessons you are meant to learn. This question invites a broader perspective on your journey, aligning your goals with the collective wisdom of your familial lineage.

Always remember to close off a scrying session by thanking the spirits and energies around you.

Perform symbolic actions with your candles, incense and any other tools that were used, extinguishing them one by one as you verbally or mentally close their corresponding energies.

Tips for Scrying Sessions

Practise patience, because connecting with your ancestors may take time.

Repeat the scrying session regularly to strengthen the connection.

Trust your instincts and maintain an open heart and mind during the process.

DIY Scrying Mirror

Materials needed:

1. A picture frame with glass
2. Window cleaner
3. Clean cloth
4. Newspaper
5. Black acrylic paint (glossy, metallic or matt)

Instructions:

Step 1: Find Your Picture Frame

Find a suitable picture frame with glass – charity shops, antique shops, second-hand stores and car-boot sales are all good places to get one. Choose a frame that resonates with you, as this will make the base of your scrying mirror.

Step 2: Clean the Glass

Use window cleaner and a clean cloth to clean the glass thoroughly, removing any streaks, smudges or fingerprints.

Step 3: Paint the Glass

Lay the cleaned glass on a piece of newspaper. Apply black acrylic paint to one side of the glass. Ideally, opt for glossy or metallic paint, although matt will work too. Ensure an even coverage with thin coats, allowing each layer to dry between applications. Approximately five or six coats are usually sufficient, or until the glass is no longer see-through when held against a source of light.

Step 4: Replace the Glass in the Frame

Once the final layer of paint is dry, place the glass back into the frame, with the painted side facing the back and the unpainted glass facing outwards.

Step 5: Reclean the Glass

Clean the glass surface one last time to eliminate any remaining streaks or smudges.

Step 6: Decorate the Frame

If desired, add magical sigils or symbols around the frame. This step is optional, but can enhance the mirror's magical properties.

Step 7: Cleanse Your Mirror

Before starting to scry with your new mirror, be sure to cleanse it of any residual energy, especially if you picked it up second-hand and it was used by someone else previously.

Remember that getting comfortable with scrying takes practice, and each scryer will have a unique approach. Feel free to experiment and discover what works best for you, although it is recommended that shorter but more frequent scrying sessions may be best to start off with. Don't forget to keep a record of your experiences and to add a few notes to your 'Book of Shadows' (see page 68) from each session.

A Reflective Journey through Nature

Pagans are known for their harmonious relationship with nature. Living in alignment and giving back to the natural world are deeply rooted in the pagan understanding of the interconnectedness of all life. This philosophy embraces the idea that humans are an integral part of a larger web of existence and, by living in this way, individuals can foster a balanced and sustainable way of life. Many pagan traditions follow a Wheel of the Year, which marks the changing seasons and the cycles of nature. Celebrations and rituals are aligned with the natural cycles of the Earth, honouring the unique qualities and energies present during each season. By celebrating the seasons, individuals seek to learn from the intricate balance found in the wild: nature becomes a teacher and guide, offering insights into spiritual growth and healing.

The Essence of Elements

One of the ways that pagans connect with the spiritual essence of the natural world is through its elements, a practice deeply intertwined with Yule celebrations. These elements are regarded as manifestations of divine energy or consciousness and are central to pagan rituals, serving as conduits for invoking or channelling spiritual energies. A widely recognized symbol representing these elements is the pentagram, a five-pointed star enclosed within a circle. Each point of the star symbolizes one of the five elements: earth, air, fire, water and spirit, while the circle represents unity, completeness and protection. Originating from ancient Mesopotamia, the pentagram gained mystical significance in Babylonian culture, where it was associated with the planets Jupiter, Mercury, Mars, Saturn and Venus. In medieval Europe it was commonly employed as a protective talisman against malevolent forces. Over time, scholars and occultists reinterpreted the pentagram, emphasizing its representation of the four elements of nature and the spiritual essence that governs them.

Understanding the importance of working with the natural elements is vital in creating a Yule celebration that is true to its origins. Equally crucial is the ability to adapt to your environment and harness its unique offerings to craft individualized magic. While snow or ice may not immediately spring to mind as magical resources, depending on your geographical location you may find yourself surrounded by one of the most potent spiritual tools without realizing it. Snow and ice have held spiritual significance in Nordic pagan traditions for as long as records exist. According to Norse mythology, the universe was created from the primordial void, called Ginnungagap. To the north of Ginnungagap lay the frozen realm of Niflheim, encapsulated by ice, cold and mist; and to the south the fiery realm of Muspelheim. The heat from Muspelheim met the cold from Niflheim, and the primordial giant Ymir and the cosmic cow Audumbla were formed. Audumbla nourished Ymir with her milk and, as she licked the salty ice of Niflheim, the god Buri, the grandfather of Odin, emerged. This tale is not only one of duality, but of the creation of life through fire and ice – a powerful recurring theme within Norse mythology.

In the present day snow continues to carry spiritual symbolism for Yule and nature-based practitioners alike. Often seen as a symbol of purity and clarity, snowfall brings about a sense of calmness, transforming bustling scenes into tranquil and still landscapes. The pristine whiteness of snow represents a blank slate, symbolizing the potential for new beginnings and the cleansing of the past. The stillness and quietness that snow brings are often associated with meditation and introspection, inviting individuals to go deeper within themselves, especially during the reflective period of Yule. On an elemental level, snow is water, which represents intuition and the ebb and flow of feelings, providing a conduit for understanding and expressing emotions. Water's natural flow, whether in rivers, springs or oceans, symbolizes the spiritual flow of energy, reminding us to go with the natural rhythm of life and to trust in the unfolding sequence of what is meant to be. Due to its purifying properties, water is also considered to have healing powers, and immersing yourself in water – in the form of baths or sacred rituals involving bodies of water – is believed to have therapeutic effects on the body, mind and spirit. Water, however, is just one of the five elements that make life on planet Earth possible. All the elements – earth, air, fire, water and spirit – should be viewed and treated as interconnected forces that collaborate to sustain life and balance the natural order of the universe.

Element	Symbolism
Earth	Grounding, stability, nourishment, foundation, fertility, endurance
Air	Communication, intellect, freedom, inspiration, clarity, breath
Fire	Transformation, passion, energy, willpower, creativity, destruction
Water	Emotions, intuition, adaptability, healing, purification, reflection
Spirit	Divine connection, unity, transcendence, oneness, spiritual essence, eternity

Incorporating snow, or even ice, into your spellwork can add a beautiful connection to the natural world. To get started on your spiritual snow work, go and gather some fresh snow or collect clean ice from a natural source and put it into a jar. If the climate is not cold enough where you live, feel free to make some ice in your freezer. Try and keep the snow or ice as clean as possible, so opt for scooping it up with your container or by using your hands. Notice where you are collecting the snow or ice from: is it new ice that has appeared overnight or a sharp icicle that has been threatening to fall for a long time? As you deepen your spiritual practice, you will begin to notice how everything has a cumulative effect, so allow your personal intuition and your interpretation of things to guide your ritual process. If you have managed to collect some snow from outside, store a container of it in your freezer and let some of it melt in a jar. You will be able to use the water from the melted snow for various different spiritual practices and rituals. Here are just a few ways in which you can use snow and ice to conduct Yuletide magic.

- **Altar elements:** Enhance your Yule altar by including a bowl or vial containing melted snow to symbolize the element of water. Place this alongside the four other classical elements, aligning each with a cardinal direction. Use a compass while standing in front of your altar to determine the north, east, south and west positions. With this guide, orient your earth element or token towards the north, position the air element facing east, let the fire element face south and, finally, direct your water element towards the west.

Earth: With the north symbolizing stability and a solid foundation, earth – associated with grounding and the material world – belongs to the north.

Air: With east being linked to the rising sun, new beginnings and the mind's awakening, air – representing intellect, communication and the realm of thought – belongs to the east.

Fire: With the south corresponding to warmth, light and the peak of the sun's power, fire – embodying transformation, passion and energy – belongs to the south.

Water: With the west associated with the setting sun, emotions and reflection, water – connected to the emotions, intuition and the subconscious – belongs to the west.

✦ **Purification spell:** Use your melted snow or ice water to cleanse a person or an object. Sprinkle on or wash the object in the water, visualizing it being cleansed and renewed. I always recommend writing your own incantations for your spellwork, but any spoken words will amplify the energy and help drive your intentions out into the universe. Here is an incantation that you can use for your spell:

> *As [person/object] bathes in nature's grace, purified now in sacred space.*
>
> *By ice and snow this spell is spun, in harmony with the winter's sun.*

- **Manifestation spell:** To perform this spell, start by writing down your desires or intentions on a piece of paper. Next, place the paper on a bed of snow or ice. You have a few options for this step: you can either leave the paper outside over time as the weather warms up and the snow begins to melt, or you can place your piece of paper on top of collected snow or ice in a jar. Alternatively, you can use ice cubes that you've made yourself; simply set one or two out in a bowl at room temperature and place your paper on top of the ice. As the snow or ice melts, visualize your intentions being released into the universe. Finally, it's recommended to return the melted water back into the earth to solidify the seed of your intention.

- **Protection spell:** We must not forget that ice and hail were so important to our German and Norse ancestors that they had their own runes to describe these elements. Refer back to Chapter 2 for the meanings of different runes, or create your own protective sigil to draw into the snow or carve into ice. Using these runes or sigils to empower your intentions, visualize forming a barrier of protection around you or your space and, in doing so, creating a shield that can deflect any unwanted energy.

- **Divination with ice cubes:** On a small piece of paper, write down the question that you need guidance on, fold it and place it in an ice-cube tray. Next, roughly crumble up some bay leaves, which are ruled by the element of fire and represent clarity and understanding, before sprinkling them into the tray. Alongside bay leaves, ideally add blue lotus-flower petals, which are associated with the element of water; these will enhance your psychic abilities and encourage spiritual enlightenment (you can buy dried lotus flowers from Etsy). However, you can substitute blue lotus flowers with any tea leaves, such as peppermint and chamomile, which are also great for increasing psychic awareness. Top your tray off with water and set it in the freezer. Once your ice cubes are frozen, cast them onto a plate, let them melt and interpret the emerging patterns for guidance. You may want to refer to a tea-reading manual for help in interpreting the placement of the lotus and bay leaves.

- **Healing spell:** Place a small item that represents healing (such as a crystal or herb) in a container and cover it with snow. As the snow melts, visualize the gradual awakening of the healing energy and the rebirth of a restored version of whatever it was that you wanted to heal.

- **Peace ritual:** Melt your snow or ice along with herbs, fruits, spices and berries in a pan, to make a simmer pot. Once infused, bottle the mixture and use it as a spray around your house to invoke a sense of peace and calmness. This also works well for purifying and cleansing spaces, and is easily customizable by adding whatever herbs, fruits and spices you choose.

- **Closure ceremony:** Begin by lighting a candle to represent the aspect of your life or situation that needs closure. Think about how that situation makes you feel, and give yourself five minutes to feel any emotions that arise. Once your five minutes are up, take a deep breath before whispering your worries to the candle, visualizing the flame absorbing your sorrows and uncertainties. When you feel ready for closure, extinguish the candle in a bowl of snow or cold water, representing the end of that chapter. The snow coming into contact with the fire not only extinguishes the flame, but also creates a new beginning, just as it created the entire universe (at least according to the Norsemen).

The Guiding Sky

As cold nights often coincide with clearer skies, Yule becomes the perfect time to stargaze and observe the cosmic glow above. Although very little information has survived from the early Norse period on the ancient Scandinavians' views on celestial bodies, we do know that they were great navigators and therefore excellent astronomers. Like other groups of people at the time, early Scandinavian inhabitants used the sun and the stars to navigate, employing the North Star to guide them at night and a type of 'sun shadow board' during the day. By the thirteenth century, old Norse constellations and their names, including the ones that were used to navigate transatlantic voyages, were replaced by Greek, Latin and Roman conceptions of the constellations.

The North Star was known by various other names, such as the 'Guiding Star' and the 'Ship's Star'; to the Old Norse, however, it was known as the 'God's Nail' and was associated with their chief deity, Thor. The star shines brightly in the night sky and is located nearly in line with the Earth's axis of rotation in the northern celestial hemisphere. It is positioned very close to the north celestial pole, which makes it appear almost stationary in the night sky, while other stars appear to revolve around it. The North Star is a part of the constellation Ursa Minor, commonly known as the Little Dipper or the Little Bear. It is often viewed as a beacon of hope, a source of guidance and, due to its fixed position, is associated with stability and constancy. Indigenous Sámi people of the north have the word *boahji*, which is related to *pohja* in Finnish, translating as not only 'north', but also 'bottom' or 'base', indicating that the Finnish word for the North Star, *pohjantähti*, is a source of foundational support.

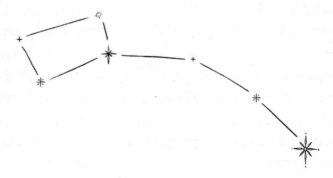

> *To make a North Star guidance jar, find a clear jar and some small stones or pebbles. As you place each stone in the jar, reflect on aspects of your life that provide stability and form the foundation of your well-being. Think of relationships, values or personal strengths. Once filled, place the jar under the night sky, preferably in view of the North Star, and let its energy charge your stones with stability and direction overnight. Whenever you feel anxious or worried, hold a pebble from the jar for a grounding and soothing effect.*

While the Sámi people consist of various different groups, each rich with its own culture, dialect and traditions, they are all united in their harmonious relationship with nature. One of the most important spirits to the Sámi is the sun. Referred to as Beaivi or Beaivvás, the sun holds a chief position among their deities and is often depicted on their shamanic drums as a central image. In the northern reaches of Finland, an ancient Sámi tradition involved baking a cake made of meal and reindeer blood, which was then placed outdoors as an offering to Beaivvás. This ritual was believed to bring good fortune to reindeer-herding and encourage the sun to shine brightly for mountain wanderers, seafarers and herders in search of lost reindeer.

Sun Crystals

As we've explored in earlier chapters, the Winter Solstice is intimately tied to the presence of the sun. This Yule deepen your connection with the sun's qualities of vitality, warmth and illumination by embracing the power of crystals. Crystals, with their unique structures and vibrational frequencies, act as natural conductors and amplifiers of energy. Different crystals are thought to resonate at different frequencies, influencing energy fields around them and enabling individuals to explore a deeper connection with the natural world and themselves. Here are a few crystals that are associated with solar energy and can help you connect with the sun and harness its spiritual properties.

- **Citrine:** Known as the 'Merchant's Stone', citrine is associated with abundance, prosperity and the energy of the sun. It is believed to bring warmth and positivity.

- **Sunstone:** This crystal is often linked to joy, success and personal power. It is believed to carry the energy of the sun and can enhance vitality and creativity.

- **Clear quartz:** As a versatile and powerful crystal, clear quartz can amplify energy and intentions. It is often used in combination with other crystals to enhance their effects.

- **Amber:** A fossilized tree resin, amber is associated with the sun's life-giving energy. It is believed to promote vitality, balance and healing.

- **Pyrite:** Known as 'Fool's Gold', pyrite resonates with the sun's energy and is associated with confidence, abundance and manifestation.

- **Tiger's eye:** This stone is linked to courage, strength and personal power. It can help channel the sun's energy for empowerment and motivation.

- **Carnelian:** A vibrant and energizing crystal, carnelian is associated with vitality, creativity and passion. It can be used to stimulate motivation and courage.

- **Yellow jasper:** The yellow hue of this crystal is associated with the sun's energy, and it is believed to bring stability, positivity and protection.

When working with these crystals to connect with the sun's energy, you can incorporate them into various practices.

- **Meditating with crystals:** Hold the crystal in your hands or place it on your solar-plexus chakra – a key energy centre in the body that is located in the upper abdomen – during meditation, to absorb the sun's energy.

- **Crystal grids:** Create a crystal grid using the selected crystals to enhance and focus the energy in a particular space. Arrange your crystals in a pattern, commonly a geometric shape, while focusing on an intention of your choosing. Activate the grid by connecting the crystals with your energy or with a wand, visualizing the energy flowing through each crystal and amplifying your intention. Leave the grid in place for as long as necessary, periodically recharging and reaffirming your intention through meditation, or affirming it with your words.

- **Wearing crystals:** Wear jewellery or carry a crystal in your pocket to keep the energy with you throughout the day.

Light and Lunar Energies

The sun wasn't the only thing to guide wanderers in the arctic darkness of Northern Europe. The Sámi traditionally believed that the Northern Lights, or aurora borealis, offered protection and a guiding light for travellers. The Finnish term for this ethereal display, *revontulet*, comes from a northern Finnish folklore in which the Northern Lights are believed to originate from the fiery tail of a fox brushing against low-hanging forest branches, creating sparks that dance across the sky. The folklore also warns against disrespecting these lights, as they were thought to comprehend speech and to condemn any misbehaviour, such as playing, laughing or throwing parties under their glow. Additionally, pointing at the Northern Lights was deemed risky, as it was believed to provide spirits with something to grasp onto, potentially spiriting the pointer away into the sky, never to return. So remember: if you find yourself under the captivating show of the Northern Lights this Yuletide, it might be best to admire it from a safe distance and refrain from inviting any mischievous spirits to your festivities!

While folklore and mythology once served as our means of conceptualizing the universe, today we embrace a more modern understanding of the cosmos, which informs our practices and fortifies our connection to various energies. A good example of this is our contemporary understanding of lunar phases. Once perceived by the Norse as the result of Mani (the moon personified) skilfully evading pursuing wolves in his chariot, we now recognize that the observable phases of the moon are shaped by the changing angles between the sun, Earth and moon. These phases include the New Moon, Waxing Crescent, First Quarter (Waxing Quarter), Waxing Gibbous, Full Moon, Waning Gibbous, Last Quarter (Waning Quarter), Waning Crescent and back to New Moon.

Spiritual work with lunar energies is often based on the belief that these lunar phases influence personal energy and consciousness. In order to foster a deeper connection with the cosmos, lunar work involves aligning intentions with the varying energies associated with each phase, from attracting and building during the waxing phase, to releasing and letting go during the waning phase. As Yule unfolds its splendour, our awareness of lunar phases deepens our awe for the ever-changing beauty of the night sky. Below are a few suggestions on how to tap into lunar energies and engage with each distinct phase of the moon during this season.

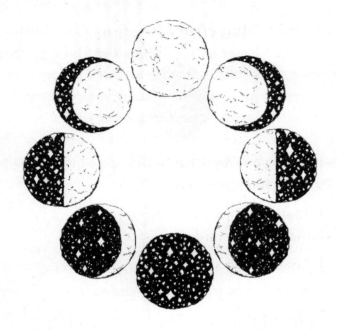

New Moon

- ✦ **Intention setting:** Use this phase to set new intentions and goals for the upcoming lunar cycle.
- ✦ **Meditation:** Practise meditation to focus on new beginnings and clarity of purpose.
- ✦ **Visualization:** Assess your current situation and envisage the manifestation of your goals.

A REFLECTIVE JOURNEY THROUGH NATURE

Waxing Crescent

- **Building energy:** Channel the growing energy to fuel your intentions.
- **Initiating projects:** Start new projects or take initial steps towards your goals.
- **Journaling:** Document your journey and progress.

First Quarter (Waxing Quarter)

- **Overcoming challenges:** Address any obstacles hindering your progress.
- **Adjusting intentions:** Reflect on your initial intentions and make adjustments, if needed.
- **Strength rituals:** Engage in rituals or practices that enhance personal strength and resolve, such as performing an affirmation

ritual, practising yoga for empowerment or participating in a guided meditation focused on inner strength and resilience.

Waxing Gibbous

+ **Refinement:** Fine-tune your goals and actions as the energy intensifies.
+ **Gratitude practice:** Express gratitude for the progress made so far.
+ **Energy healing:** Focus on energy-healing practices for balance.

Full Moon

+ **Culmination:** The Full Moon is a time for the culmination of energy and intentions.

- ✦ **Release:** Let go of what no longer serves you through rituals such as Full Moon releases, where you write down whatever you wish to release or let go of and then burn or bury it, as a symbolic gesture of releasing it from your life. This can include negative thought patterns, habits, fears or anything else that is holding you back from personal growth and fulfilment.
- ✦ **Divination:** Engage in divination practices for guidance.

Waning Gibbous

- ✦ **Harvesting energy:** Spend time in nature to absorb and ground all the lunar energy generated during waxing phases.
- ✦ **Reflection:** Reflect on the lessons learned and acknowledge achievements.
- ✦ **Energy cleansing:** Perform cleansing rituals to release residual energies.

Last Quarter (Waning Quarter)

- **Release and forgiveness:** Let go of any lingering negative energies or resentments.
- **Shadow work:** Delve into deeper aspects of the self through shadow work.
- **Meditative practices:** Embrace quiet, introspective practices.

Waning Crescent

- **Rest and recharge:** Focus on self-care and rejuvenation.
- **Dreamwork:** Pay attention to dreams and messages from your subconscious.

- **Preparation:** Make space for new intentions, ready for the New Moon, by doing some scrapbooking or journaling to organize your thoughts and clear mental clutter.

New Moon (again)

- **Setting new intentions:** Begin the cycle anew by setting fresh intentions.
- **Cleansing rituals:** Purify your space and energy for a new beginning.
- **Vision-board creation:** Craft a vision board to represent your goals.

To use the moon for cleansing and charging, place your items under the light of the Full Moon, which is particularly potent for this purpose as it symbolizes culmination and illumination. Whether it's crystals, spiritual tools such as tarot cards or personal objects, allow them to bask in the moonlight overnight. As you set them out, focus on your intention to cleanse away any negative energies and charge them with the pure, transformative energy of the Full Moon. Retrieve your items the next morning, feeling a sense of renewal and enhanced energy within them. This simple and long-standing practice harnesses the moon's natural energy cycles to support spiritual and energetic well-being in your chosen objects.

You can also make moon water by placing a container of water under the light of the Full Moon and leaving it there overnight. Moon water is believed to absorb the lunar energy and can be used for various spiritual practices, such as cleansing crystals, tools or spaces, as well as incorporating it into rituals, meditation and energetic cleansing practices. Remember that, while the moon's phases provide a rhythmic and cyclical framework for self-reflection and growth, your spiritual journey and practices are unique to you, so spend some time reflecting on what each phase of the moon means for you. Think about what kind of emotions each phase evokes in you, and see if you can spot any patterns that emerge in your life throughout the month as the moon waxes and wanes.

Whispering Woodlands and Their Inhabitants

Based on the sacred relationship between pagans and nature, many neo-pagans believe that various natural elements, both visible and invisible, are conscious. This includes everything from trees, rocks and rivers to animals, fire and even constructed features such as stone circles and ancient temples. Forests and trees in particular hold immense significance for Nordic pagans and are deeply intertwined with their culture and spiritual beliefs.

In Nordic mythology the symbolism of trees extends to the concept of Yggdrasil, the World Tree. Yggdrasil is a colossal and sacred ash tree that serves as the cosmic axis, connecting different realms of existence. In Norse cosmology, trees were not merely physical entities, but were believed to harbour spiritual essence and wisdom. Individuals seeking guidance or enlightenment would often commune with trees, especially ancient and majestic ones. Historically, sacred groves were places of worship for the Norse, where specific trees, or clusters of them, were deemed holy. These groves served as outdoor sanctuaries for rituals, ceremonies and communal gatherings, fostering a sense of unity with nature and the divine. This connection with sacred groves has influenced modern practices, encouraging individuals to seek out or create their own sacred spaces in natural settings. Here are some other ways, inspired by Nordic paganism, in which you can connect with trees and the energies of the forest.

- **Tree meditation:** Engage in meditation near a tree, visualizing roots extending into the earth and branches reaching into the sky. Seek guidance and wisdom from the tree's spirit.

- **Tree rituals:** Conduct rituals honouring specific trees or the archetype of Yggdrasil. Offerings can include water, seeds or handmade items as symbols of reciprocity.

- **Tree symbolism:** Study the symbolic meanings of different trees in Norse mythology. For example, the ash tree represents the interconnectedness of all life, while the oak is associated with strength and protection.

- **Tree divination:** Practise divination or seek insights by observing the shapes of leaves, patterns in bark or the direction of branches. This method, known as dendromancy, involves interpreting messages from the trees.

- **Sacred groves:** Create or visit sacred groves, areas dedicated to nature worship. These spaces can serve as sanctuaries for rituals, meditation and fostering a deeper connection with the spiritual energy of trees.

The deep-green forests of the north were also home to various different animals that became an integral part of the spiritual landscape of Nordic pagans. Animals such as deer, wolves and birds played crucial roles in mythology and were seen as messengers or embodiments of divine forces. For instance, hares were often associated with the birth of life, as well as the concept of intuition. Other examples of forest animals and their symbolic meanings to early Nordic pagans include:

- **Wolf:** Wolves were revered for their fierce yet cunning nature. In Norse mythology the wolf was associated with the god Odin, who had two wolf companions, Geri and Freki. Wolves embodied both danger and wisdom, reflecting the dualistic nature of the wild and the inherent balance between chaos and order.

- **Deer:** The deer, particularly the majestic stag, symbolized strength and renewal. The stag was associated with the woodland realm and often represented the close connection between the natural world and the divine. In some myths the stag was seen as a guide through the spiritual realms.

- **Raven**: The raven held significant symbolism in Norse mythology, being particularly associated with the god Odin. Two ravens, Huginn (thought) and Muninn (memory), served as Odin's messengers. Ravens were considered highly intelligent birds, embodying wisdom, communication between worlds and the ability to access hidden knowledge.

- **Bear**: Bears were seen as powerful and protective beings, associated with the warrior spirit. The bear symbolized strength, courage and ferocity in battle. Some Norse warriors invoked the spirit of the bear for strength and resilience in times of conflict.

- **Fox**: Foxes were seen as cunning and sly, embodying both cleverness and adaptability. In Norse folklore the fox was sometimes associated

- **Boar**: Respected for their strength and ferocity in battle, boars were associated with the god Freyr, representing fertility and abundance.

Embark on an enchanting journey to uncover your animal spirit guide through a forest meditation. Prepare for this immersive experience by gathering cosy attire and a comfortable blanket to sit on, as you head to your favourite woodland spot. As you journey to the forest, consider inviting a companion to join you, perhaps someone to recite the meditation as you immerse yourself in the tranquil surroundings. Prepare to step into nature's sacred haven and connect with your animal spirit guide amid the serene embrace of the forest.

To start your spirit-guide meditation, gently close your eyes, inhale a few deep breaths and immerse yourself in the vision of being surrounded by the lush woodland. Imagine yourself strolling through an ancient forest adorned with emerald-green trees and, as the sun filters through the leaves, witness the subtle sparkle they exude. Allow your senses to awaken to the sounds, scents and sensations around you. Envision the forest stirring to life, and, as you navigate its winding paths, invite various animals to join you on your walk. Some creatures may approach with curiosity, before gracefully retreating to their sanctuaries. Observe their behaviour keenly, noting any creature that resonates with you or imparts a sense of familiarity. Has a particular animal chosen to accompany you, walking by your side?

If no animal approaches, spend a few moments grounding yourself with the palms of your hands pressed against the earth.

Inhale deeply, envisioning the essence of the forest infusing your being and, with each exhale, release any tension or worries. Allow the natural energy of the woodland to guide you deeper into a state of calm presence. With your senses attuned to the enchanted surroundings, visualize a gentle mist weaving through the trees. This mist holds the potential to unveil your animal spirit guide. Picture it swirling into a soft form before you. As the mist takes shape, notice the emergence of an animal companion, its spirit gleaming with curiosity. Observe its size, colour and the energy it emanates. Trust your instincts: this creature has chosen to reveal itself to guide you. When you feel a sense of completion, express your gratitude to the animal spirit guide for sharing its wisdom. Watch as the mist begins to dissipate, returning to the embrace of the forest.

As you conclude your journey into the depths of the forest, feeling refreshed and spiritually connected, continue to celebrate the harmony between humans and the natural world. Inspired by the pagan Yule tradition of giving back to nature, why not extend a gesture of kindness to our avian friends by crafting a charming DIY bird-feeder? Take this sweet eco-friendly creation with you on your next woodland walk or hang it in your garden to attract flying visitors to your magical sanctuary. So as you prepare to return from your enchanted forest meditation, bring along the materials for this simple yet meaningful project and spread the joy of Yule to your little feathered friends.

DIY Natural Bird-Feeder

Materials needed:

1. Pine cones (gather a few large ones, so that you have a few to choose from)

2. Peanut butter or sunflower butter (opt for a natural, organic and unsweetened variety with as few additives as possible; I prefer Meridian's Smooth Peanut Butter, which contains only whole roasted peanuts without any added salt)
3. Birdseed (choose a mix that suits the local bird species)
4. String or twine, for hanging the feeders
5. Butter knife or spoon, to spread the peanut butter
6. Plate or tray, to catch any birdseed

Instructions:

Step 1: Prepare Your Work Area

Lay out a plate or tray to catch any birdseed that may fall during the crafting process.

Step 2: Choose Your Pine Cones

Large, open pine cones will provide ample space for spreading the peanut butter and attaching the birdseed.

Step 3: Cut a Piece of String or Twine

Tie one end of the string or twine securely around the top of each pine cone.

Step 4: Spread the Nut Butter

Using a butter knife or spoon, spread a generous layer of nut butter onto each pine cone. Ensure that it covers the gaps between the cone's scales, creating a sticky surface for the birdseed.

Step 5: Coat the Pine Cone

Roll the nut-butter-coated pine cones in birdseed, pressing gently to help the seeds adhere. Rotate each pine cone to cover it evenly with the birdseed, ensuring that all the nut butter is concealed.

Step 6: Cover the Entire Surface

If there are any bare spots, apply more nut butter and roll them in birdseed until the entire surface is covered.

Step 7: Allow to Set

Let the bird-feeders sit for a little while to allow the nut butter to set and adhere firmly to the pine cones.

Step 8: Find a Hanging Spot

Once the bird-feeders are ready, find a suitable spot to hang them. You can use the attached string or twine to secure them to branches or hooks.

Step 9: Enjoy Your Bird-Feeder

Sit back and observe the delightful array of birds that visit your home-made feeder. Different bird species may be attracted, depending on the type of birdseed used.

As the seasons shift and winter blankets the landscape during Yule, forest animals, ranging from squirrels to birds, find sustenance in an array of natural offerings. Nordic berries, such as lingonberries, cloudberries, cranberries and bilberries, have been vital for both humans and forest inhabitants alike throughout time. For forest animals, some of these berries serve as a vital source of nutrition when other food options are scarce, ensuring their survival during colder periods. While certain kinds of berries have disappeared and been consumed by wildlife before the first frost covers the ground, others are not eaten by wildlife until after they have frozen over, because the cold lowers the bitterness and acidity of the berries. For us humans, these vibrant offerings of nature see communities come together to preserve and turn them into jams, jellies and syrups to stave off the winter blues and boost immunity. It is very common for neighbours to make preserves using frozen berries picked earlier on in the year and then gift them within the neighbourhood in the days leading up to Yule.

Spiritual and Symbolic Associations with Nordic Berries

- **Cranberries:** These crimson jewels of the forest are vibrant in colour and tart in flavour, evoking feelings of vitality and renewal. Often associated with the bountiful harvests of autumn, cranberries mark the transition from light into darkness when they appear. Their tartness is said to awaken the senses and invigorate the spirit, making them a staple ingredient in traditional Yule dishes and beverages. Beyond their culinary uses, cranberries are also seen as symbols of protection and prosperity in Nordic folklore. It is believed that hanging cranberry garlands around the home or wearing them as jewellery can ward off evil spirits and bring good fortune in the coming year.

- **Lingonberries:** These berries symbolize the harmony and interconnectedness of all things and have played a significant role in Nordic culture for centuries. Their evergreen leaves signify eternal life, and the red berries embody the lifeblood that sustains both humans and the natural world. In the Finnish epic *Kalevala* the story of the Virgin Marjatta adds layers to the lingonberry's symbolism. Marjatta, a young maiden, becomes impregnated by a lingonberry and gives birth to Kullervo, her son. Kullervo's tumultuous life, fraught with hardship and misfortune, embodies the tragic hero-archetype in Finnish folklore. This narrative contributes to the lingonberry's association with fertility and life force. The lingonberry's resilience in harsh conditions also mirrors the strength required by those living in cold climates, and therefore makes the perfect charm or amulet for protection.

- **Bilberries:** Bilberries are often associated with intuition, wisdom and the mysteries of the unseen. Their deep-purple colour signifies spiritual insight and the unfolding of hidden truths. Bilberries are linked to shamanic practices in Nordic cultures and are believed to enhance spiritual vision and facilitate communication with the spirit realm. In rituals, bilberries are sometimes consumed to heighten awareness and deepen a connection with the unseen forces.

- **Cloudberries:** These are considered a symbol of enlightenment and transformation. Their golden colour represents the sun and the illumination of spiritual knowledge; hence they are the perfect addition to your Yule celebrations. Cloudberries are also associated with good fortune and prosperity. Believed to be the food of the goddess Freyja, their presence in rituals signifies the pursuit of wisdom and the journey towards spiritual enlightenment.

Today, we can draw inspiration from the berries of the north and their spiritual properties to add a touch of Nordic magic into our daily lives. A delightful way to do this is to make your own personalized mix of Berry Bath Salts, which also makes a perfect, thoughtful Yule gift. Don't forget to treat yourself to a spiritual bath, or leave a note with some tips on how to set one up, to give with your gift. Here is a simple DIY guide.

Make your own Berry Bath Salts

Ingredients:

- ¼ cup dried Nordic berries (found in most healthfood stores): you can dry your own or use pre-dried berry powder

- 1 cup Epsom salts
- ½ cup sea salt
- 10–15 drops of essential oil (such as juniper or lavender)

Instructions:

1. Dry your chosen berries using one of the methods below or use pre-dried berry powder.

   Oven drying: Preheat your oven to the lowest setting (usually around 50°C on a fan setting) and place a parchment-lined tray of berries (in a single layer) inside, with the door slightly ajar to allow the moisture to escape. The drying time in the oven typically ranges from four to twelve hours, depending on the berries' type and size. It's advisable to check regularly and rotate the trays, for even drying.

   Dehydrator: Follow the manufacturer's instructions for drying berries in a food dehydrator.

   Your berries are ready when they have a slightly shrivelled appearance and are no longer soft. It's crucial to ensure that they are thoroughly dried, to prevent mould or spoilage during storage.

2. Grind the dried berries into a coarse powder.
3. In a bowl, mix the Epsom salts, sea salt and berry powder together.
4. Add the essential oils to the mixture and blend well.
5. Transfer the blend into a decorative jar or pouch.

Tips for a Yule-Berry Bath

Prepare for your spiritual Yule-berry bath by setting the atmosphere with candles and music. Choose citrus-scented candles for a morning bath to invigorate your senses, and opt for mahogany-infused ones for an evening bath to create a relaxing ambience.

Once the mood is set, add a generous handful of berry-infused bath salts to your warm bath water. As you soak, take the time to reflect on the symbolic meanings and restorative properties of the berries.

Embrace the quiet moments of solitude, allowing the water to wash away not only physical impurities, but also the mental and emotional residue of everyday life. Let the aroma of the essential oils calm your mind, body and soul.

When it's time to drain the water from your bath, envision any tension and stress also draining from your body.

Take a few moments for post-bath contemplation, and journal any thoughts and feelings that arose during the process.

Final Thoughts

As our journey through Yule draws to a close, it prompts us to reflect on the profound message at the heart of this season. Yule is, fundamentally, about connection – a deep intertwining with nature, with the elemental forces, with our communities and, most importantly, with ourselves. It's a period of profound introspection, when delving into the depths of our being reveals that we hold the power to shape our realities. This season of self-discovery invites us to tap into our inner wisdom, intuition and creative potential, empowering us to manifest our deepest desires and dreams. Embracing the lessons of Yule reminds us of the interconnectedness of all existence, and of our pivotal role as co-creators of our lives and the world around us. By nurturing this deep connection with ourselves and the universe, we cultivate a sense of inner peace, fulfilment and meaning, ultimately enriching our lives with profound purpose.

Understanding the essence of cultivating a magical practice is a deeply personal journey, as unique as each individual. It's about delving into the depths of our beliefs, values and experiences to discover what resonates with our souls. When embarking on this spiritual exploration, I always advocate following your curiosity and intuition. Whether it's a fascination with crystals, a passion for stargazing or the joy found in cooking… the signs are already there, just waiting to be noticed. There is no pre-defined path to adhere to; it's about uncovering what ignites your curiosity and brings you joy and fulfilment, even if it means embracing discomfort along the way, for there lies the potential for important lessons and revelations.

Identifying as spiritual is not about fitting into a predetermined mould, and no specific appearance or environment is required in order to embrace magical practices. It's about honouring your intuition, following your heart and discovering routines and rituals that nourish your spirit, especially during the winter season, which is filled with opportunities for reflection. Whether it's through meditation, prayer, communing with nature or any other form of self-expression, authenticity and alignment with your true self are key.

As we rejoice in the increasing light after the Winter Solstice, amid the darkest season of the year, Yule serves as an important reminder of the dual energies that constantly prevail in our lives. Symbolizing both expansion and contraction, Yule beckons us to embrace new insights and perspectives and to transcend limitations, while simultaneously delving deeper within ourselves for inner healing. Moreover, Yule embodies a paradoxical essence of creation and destruction – it is a testament to the cyclical nature of birth, death and rebirth. Creation is the source of life and abundance, embodying the power to bring about new beginnings, growth and manifestation, yet it necessitates the dissolution of old structures in order to allow novel things to flourish. Yuletide is therefore the perfect time to focus on releasing old patterns and attachments that no longer serve our highest good, clearing the way for fresh growth. Ultimately Yule invites us to honour the equilibrium of opposing forces, embracing the lessons of the past, all the while looking forward to the new beginnings and opportunities that lie ahead.

As the waning year surrenders to the commanding darkness, turn to some of the tools discussed in this book to seek protection and joy on your journey. Illuminate your path with the flickering glow of candles, activate your sigils, lace your meals with magic and cast your runes. Remember to pay homage to those who paved the way before you, and to engage in ancestry work to forge connections with your familial lineage. Performing ancestry work and connecting with your family during Yule are not only beautiful ways to connect with your magical craft, but to draw upon their guidance and blessings for the new year ahead. By honouring the customs and teachings of your forebears you can deepen your sense of cultural identity and spiritual connection, shaping your unique journey and your quest to find purpose.

As you have journeyed through Nordic pagan Yuletide traditions and have reimagined the enchantment of the holiday season, a world of possibilities awaits you beyond these pages. Before we part ways, I give you one final reflection: always strive to look beyond the surface, in search of hidden truths. By looking past superficial first impressions we open ourselves to unexpected connections and infinite possibilities. Whether it's travelling through time to explore the origins of Christmas, unravelling the mysteries of the natural world or contemplating the vastness of the universe, the act of looking beyond what is immediately visible ignites our curiosity and expands our understanding. It's in this realm of exploration that we find enlightenment, growth and the true essence of life's beauty.

And should you ever doubt your intrinsic power or significance, remember this: from the intricate patterns of a snowflake to the vast expanse of the cosmos, the same celestial elements that make up distant stars flow through your veins – making you, my dear friend, extraordinary.

Acknowledgements

As the winter winds whisper secrets of the season, I find myself filled with gratitude for those who have walked this enchanting path with me.

To my editor, Erika, thank you for your steadfast dedication and unwavering belief in this project. Your keen eye, insightful guidance and profound understanding of my vision has transformed this book into a true celebration of Yule's wonders.

A heartfelt thanks to my illustrator, Lauren. Your breathtaking artistry has brought the magic of this book to life in a way words alone never could, and I am endlessly grateful for your creative brilliance and vision.

To my family, my eternal circle of strength and love, your support has been the spellbinding force behind this creation. Your enthusiasm and words of encouragement have illuminated the way through each chapter.

This book is a testament to the collective magic we share, together we have conjured something truly special. Thank you for being part of this winter's tale.